Elusive Dom

Kaci Rose

Five Little Roses Publishing

Copyright

Publisher's Note: This is a work of fiction. Names, characters, places, and incidents are a product of the author's imagination. Locales and public names are sometimes used for atmospheric purposes. Any resemblance to actual people, living or dead, or to businesses, companies, events, institutions, or locales is completely coincidental.

Book Cover By: **Sarah Kil Creative Studio**

Editing By: Debbe @ **On The Page, Author and PA Services**

Proofreads by: Laura B. and Ashley at **All Things Geeky Girl**

Contents

Get Free Books! VII
1. Chapter 1 1
2. Chapter 2 9
3. Chapter 3 21
4. Chapter 4 31
5. Chapter 5 41
6. Chapter 6 55
7. Chapter 7 63
8. Chapter 8 71
9. Chapter 9 81
10. Chapter 10 91
11. Chapter 11 97
12. Chapter 12 105
13. Chapter 13 115
14. Chapter 14 129
15. Chapter 15 139

16. Chapter 16 151
17. Chapter 17 161
18. Chapter 18 173
19. Chapter 19 185
20. Chapter 20 193
21. Chapter 21 209
22. Chapter 22 221
23. Chapter 23 231
24. Chapter 24 243
25. Chapter 25 251
26. Chapter 26 257
27. Chapter 27 265
28. Chapter 28 271
29. Chapter 29 281
30. Chapter 30 287
31. Epilogue 295
32. Other Books by Kaci Rose 301
33. Connect with Kaci Rose 307
34. About Kaci Rose 309
35. Please Leave a Review! 311

Get Free Books!

Do you like Military Men? Best friends brothers?
What about sweet, sexy, and addicting books?

If you join Kaci Rose's Newsletter you get these books free!

https://www.kacirose.com/free-books/

Now on to the story!

Chapter 1

Gemma

What in the hell was I thinking?

My new roommate thought it would be a great idea for me to get my mind off my now ex-fiancé, Dustin. She said she knew exactly what I needed and had the perfect night out planned. I should have asked more questions.

We're now standing outside the famous Club Red sex club in downtown Chicago. It looks more like a warehouse, but that's not what is putting me off. It's more the fact that this is where my best friend hooked up with my dad several months ago.

She is now my new stepmother, and they are happy together. I love them both, but my dad is a member here."I can't go in there," I tell my roommate, Skye.

"Why the hell not?" She says, tucking her keys into her purse.

"Because my dad is a member here," I tell her like it's the most obvious thing in the world. Because to me, it is. There is no way I can go into the same sex club where my dad is a member.

"Well, he and Summer are going to see that new movie tonight. I verified they would not be here, so there's no reason that you can't go in there."

Summer and I were roommates before she got together with my dad, so I'm not surprised that Skye checked with her beforehand. I don't want to admit that curiosity seems to want to get the better of me. I do want to know what the allure is and why Skye is a regular member here.

I also want to know why Summer is always raving about it. She's been telling me I should go, but I keep putting it off.

"Come on, you read the same books I do, and I know that you're curious. I think that you're going to like it. It'll be the best rebound you can have."

"But I don't need a rebound because I was the one to call off the engagement," I remind her.

"But you guys were together for a while, so you need a rebound."

I don't think I need a rebound. I called off the engagement because I was more excited when my dad and Summer got engaged than I was over my engagement. That pretty much said everything.

Plus, my dad was a single dad since I was six. When my mother died, he worked his butt off and was the most amazing parent I could ever ask for. We're close, and the fact that Dustin didn't even think to ask for my dad's blessing or even talk to my dad before proposing just didn't sit right with me.

"Look, here are the car keys. You can leave anytime you want. I've got a few people here I can catch a ride with. Just promise me you'll give it at least thirty minutes. Go in, have a drink, and look around. Check out both the first and second floors. If you don't like it, you can bolt," Skye says.

My curiosity is definitely getting the better of me. Skye has talked about Club Red before, and I want to see what all the hype is about. So, taking a deep breath, I nod my head. Now hopefully, I'm prepared to walk in the door.

She takes my hand and guides me up to the glass doors that you can't see through from the street. I was expecting it to look like a sex club from the moment I stepped inside. But what I wasn't expecting was a clean, bright lobby that looks like it belongs in some kind of modern office building.

Standing here, you would never know that on the other side of the big leather double doors sits one of Chicago's most notorious BDSM clubs. There's a dull thump from the music bass on the other side. By the doors, there are two men standing, while another man is guarding a small white door. It looks like a door that could lead to any simple room in any house on the other side of the wall.

"Gemma," Skye says, getting my attention.

"Here you go, dear, just fill this out," the receptionist says all sweet as she and Skye go back to talking.

Sitting down on one of the white leather chairs, I look at the form. It states that Skye is sponsoring me for a thirty-day guest membership.

We had filled out a lot of this online when we sent in my doctor's physical and the STD test I had to have, along with the proof that I am on birth control. Then I was required to fill out a series of consent and liability forms all of which they make me go over again now just to be sure.

Reading further, there's the list of rules I have to initial next to each one. Don't interrupt other people's scenes. Stop doesn't mean stop. Red is the only code word that means stop. It goes over the club's safe words like green means you're ready to go with the scene or happy with how the scene is going. Yellow, you're coming up to a limit or you're pushing against a limit. When you say red, the scene comes to a complete end. Consent is stressed constantly over and over again. Even having to consent to touch someone. It doesn't matter if it's something as simple as holding their hand.

For our protection, there are plain-clothed monitors and security members everywhere, along with security personnel who are easily identified. Many paragraphs are filled with details of what to do if a scene goes wrong, the consequences for breaking the rules, and everything in between. The more I read through the paperwork, the more comforting it is to know that there are rules in place to protect me. It makes me more secure knowing there are people in place who will ensure I'll be safe.

Finally, I turn in the clipboard with my signatures on it, and give my ID card to the receptionist. A few minutes later, she hands me a very discrete member's card. It's a deep red with the word 'membership' at the top with a member number, and on the back is a bar code. It doesn't have my name or mention of the club, so I'm guessing if it's ever found, there's no way to link me to Club Red other than in their system.

"Does she need a tour, or will you handle that, Skye?" the receptionist asks.

"I got this thanks," she says and then leads me through the simple white door, which opens into a hallway.

"Let's put your stuff in a locker in the locker room next to the restrooms. At the other end of the hall are all the security and the club owner's offices."

She guides me into a locker room where almost everything is white. We put our things in the locker, which takes our fingerprint as our key. It's high-tech stuff that I've never seen before.

Once everything is in our lockers, she walks us back into the lobby and through the leather doors. Stepping into the main area of the club is like entering a completely different planet.

The room still has the old warehouse feel with cement floors, but it's a wide-open space.

"There's a two-drink maximum, but you can have all the water you want. They also have snack foods and finger foods at the bar," she says. Then she points to the other side of the room where the largest bar I've ever seen, with over twenty bar stools, is sitting.

This club does nothing small because in front of us is the largest black leather with red accents sectional coach that I've ever seen. It's so large it could easily hold over twenty people and there are large ottomans scattered in front of it big enough to hold three or four people lying down. More if they're sitting up.

The lights are low, but as my eyes start to adjust, I take a look round. My eyes land on the stage at the far end of the room where a couple is performing. Others stop and watch for a moment and go on with their business, while some sit and watch intently.

"The archway to the left of the bar leads to the voyeur hall. All sorts of different themed rooms are located there, and as long as the curtains are open, you're free to watch." She points to an archway to the left of the bar.

"The second floor has themed and private rooms. Also, there's a smaller intimate lounge area where you can watch things down here, as long as the doors and windows are open." She points to the wall of glass above us.

It reminds me of a hotel lobby I was in with my dad on one family vacation except there's no hallway and balcony. It's just a wall of glass. Some you can see into and others you can't.

"What's on the third floor?" I ask, looking at the row of glass that you can't see into at all.

"Those are the VIP suites. They're the ones who pay every month to have a private suite. The owners also have a suite up there. You can't get to that floor unless you're invited, so only worry about the first and second floors. Now, let's get you a drink because trust me, you are going to need one."

Skye pulls me toward the bar and orders me a Malibu coconut rum and pineapple juice, my go-to drink.

I take a sip and turn on the bar stool to look at the room.

"Hey, I see a friend. You okay or do you need me to stay with you?" Skye asks.

"I'm good. I think I'm going to sit here and just watch," I tell her, motioning her off.

Taking a minute, I look around the room. There are several couples on the couch, a woman tied to the Saint Andrews cross beside the couch, and a man playing with the woman strapped to the cross. On one of the ottomans, a woman is sitting on a man's face and I can only imagine what's going on based on her look of pure ecstasy.

People here are letting everything hang out, while others are mostly covered in lingerie. I seem to be very overdressed in my tiny skintight dress, which is less clothes than I've ever worn. I'm extremely uncomfortable in this dress with how much is showing.

As I take another sip from my drink, a man in a suit sits down next to me.

"Are you new here?" he asks. His deep tone sends tingles across my skin.

"Yes, a friend of mine brought me as a guest. She's over there talking to some friends." I nod in the direction where Skye is.

Turning to get a good look at the man next to me, my eyes widen. Fuck, is he gorgeous. A few gray hairs at his temples, but otherwise dark brown hair. There are some wrinkle lines at the corners of his eyes. If I had to guess, I'd say he's in his late thirties. But then again, I've always been attracted to men older than me. I think it's because they are more mature than the immature little boys that are my age.

"Do you like what you see?" he asks, catching me off guard.

Chapter 2
Carter

Even in this light, I can tell her face flushes red. And fuck if it's not the cutest thing I've ever seen. Even my cock agrees. It's getting hard at just the sight of the red on her cheeks.

Normally, I don't flirt with women here. I do my business and leave, but for some reason, I just can't seem to walk away from her.

"What's your name?"

"Gemma."

"Well, Gemma. I'm Carter. Do you see anything you like?" Taking a chance, I push my luck and ask her again.

She looks around again but doesn't say anything. Finally, she nods. I'll take it. It's better than nothing.

"May I touch you?" I don't know why I'm asking. I shouldn't want to play with her. But I know there's no way in hell I'll be able to walk away.

Again, she nods.

When I run the back of my finger slowly down her arm, I love the way that her breathing quickens and how her skin pebbles beneath my touch.

"What do you see looking around the room that you like the most?" I ask, while still slowly running my finger over her arm.

Her eyes look around the room, but they keep darting to the stage. Then she quickly looks away, as if she's embarrassed to like what she sees.

On the stage is a sub tied to a Saint Andrew's cross and her dom is sharing her with other men.

"Look at the woman on stage. Don't take your eyes off of her."

She does as I ask, which makes me even harder knowing that she obeys so sweetly.

As she watches her nipples pebble beneath the thin dress she has on.

"You know your safe words, right?" I ask before moving on.

"Yes," she says breathlessly.

"What are they?" I want to be sure.

"Green means I'm good, yellow I'm getting close to a limit, and red means stop."

"Good girl. What color are you now?"

"Green," she says, and I smile.

She has to be nervous, but she isn't letting it control her, and I will reward her for that. Still, one more question before we move on.

"Do you want to play with me tonight?" Asking for her consent is of utmost importance to me.

Her eyes lock with mine. She takes the time to think about it and not just throw out an answer. I appreciate that she's cautious and careful.

"Yes," she says, her eyes never leaving my face.

I let out the breath I didn't even realize I was holding. The fact that utter disappointment would have filled me if she had said no is something I can unpack later. Resting my hand on her knee, I watch for her reaction as I slowly slide my hand up the inside of her leg.

Her breathing picks up and I start to wonder if the skin-on-skin contact is doing the same thing to her as it is to me. I may only be able to feel her skin with the tips of my fingers, but it's like I can feel it all over my body. My cock is hard and throbbing. As my hand slips under her skirt, she tenses but doesn't tell me to stop, so I pause, giving her time to process before I run my finger over her soaked panties.

Something snaps inside of me, and I want to explore her. Gently taking her hand, I help her off the barstool and we walk across the room to the couch. Sitting down, I pull her onto my lap, with her back to my chest, and her perfect ass nestled against my cock.

"What do you see that you like?" I ask while moving my hands down her sides to her hips. When she starts wiggling against me, I tighten my grip on her hips and hold her still.

Still looking around the room, I see her staring at a couple at one end of the couch. The woman is still fully dressed, and the man is taking her roughly from behind. While her gaze is riveted on them, I let my hands continue to travel down her legs.

I hook her legs on the outside of mine and then spread them open. She's exposed to anyone walking by, but her underwear is keeping her covered. Then, using one hand to hold her in place, I use the other to brush lightly over her panty covered clit. She moans, and I can feel the vibration throughout my body.

Slipping my fingers inside her panties, I coat them in her juices before playing with her clit some more.

"What about what's happening on the stage?" I redirect her attention to the new show on the stage where a woman is tied and being held down, while her partner is sharing her with several other men.

As I slowly stroke her clit, one man finishes and the next one steps up to take his place. It's then her pussy gushes.

"What part of that made you so excited?" When she doesn't answer me, I halt my movements. Right away, she answers.

"Them sharing her," she says, her voice shaky.

"Is that something you'd be interested in? Being shared?" I ask as I slowly restart my movements on her clit.

"I've only read about it, but I'd be interested," she says, letting her head fall back against my shoulder.

I play and bring her right to the edge before removing my hands and pulling her dress down to cover her back up. She lets out a whimper and lifts her head to look at me.

"The first time you cum will be on my tongue and the second time will be on my cock. If you still want this, we can head upstairs." I wait for her to make a decision.

"Yes," she says, still trying to catch her breath.

Gently, I help her stand. Then taking her hand, I lead her upstairs. We easily could have taken the elevator, but selfishly, I want to watch her climb the stairs in that dress. It's short enough that I get a hint of what's beneath it.

When we reach the second floor, she turns to look at me. I guess she expects me to pick a room here.

"Up one more flight, baby girl," I tell her, making her eyes go wide.

It seems her friend has given her the lowdown of what's on the third floor. At least as far as what her friend knows. One perk of owning the club is having my private room, not that I've taken advantage of it much.

Once we reach the top of the stairs, I take her hand and lead her down to my room. I open the door and step aside to allow her in then close and lock the door behind me.

"Wow. This room is amazing," she says.

But she doesn't ask any questions, and I'm glad because I'm not sure I want to answer any tonight.

She makes her way to the huge wall of windows that looks out over what's happening below and stands staring down there.

"Can they see up here?" she asks.

"No, and I can close the windows altogether if it makes you more comfortable," I tell her, not moving from my space in front of the door.

She turns to look at me, giving me a shy smile. "I think I'd like that."

Nodding, I turn to the panel and with the push of a button, the windows turn black, and you can no longer see out of them.

She looks around the rest of the room, taking everything in.

On one wall there's an oversized bed. There are dressers and display shelves full of things with which to play. Across from the bed is a Saint Andrew's cross. In one corner, there's a desk that I sometimes come up to work at and get away from everybody. There's a small mini-bar with refreshments and snacks as well.

After she finishes perusing the room, her eyes land back on me.

It's time for me to take charge. "Your safe words still work here. You say red and everything stops," I remind her.

She nods.

"Remove your dress and lay down in the middle of the bed," I say in my dom voice that has not been used in a long time.

She hesitates, and I wait to see what she does. Finally, she turns and walks towards the bed, stopping at the side. It's our first night together and she's allowed to be nervous. But if this goes any further than tonight, she'll learn that I won't stand for any hesitation.

Slowly she removes her dress, revealing that she was not wearing a bra underneath. Now the only thing she has on are her lace panties.

Taking off my suit jacket, I place it on the desk. Then I unbutton my cuffs and roll up my sleeves. As I make my way to the bed, she watches my every move.

When I'm standing beside the bed, she turns toward me and walks over on her knees, placing a hand on my shoulder. She's about to learn I'm the one in control and that means I'm not to be touched.

I take her wrists and guide her back to the center of the bed and lay her down. Then I stretch her arms out and lock them in the handcuffs that are already in place. They are ones that I had built into the bed.

Once she's secure, I look her over. Normally I'd blindfold her, but there is something about her that makes me not want to. I like the feeling of her eyes on me and that's new for me. Not only do I want her to see me, but I want to be able to see her.

"What color are you at, baby girl?" I ask, moving to the front of the bed.

"Green."

"I won't ask again. It's your job to tell me if that changes. Understood?"

"Yes."

"Sir," I add.

She catches on quickly.

"Yes, Sir," she says.

My already hard cock pulses at her obedience.

Climbing on the bed, I pull her panties down, while my eyes stay on her face watching for any sign she's changing her mind. All I see is desire, so I get in a position to make good on my promise. I gently run my hands up her thighs, pushing her legs open and getting the first look at her pussy, which is glistening with desire for me. That alone is a turn-on.

When I run my thumb over her clit, her body jerks against the restraints.

Going for broke, I take my first lick of her. The tangy flavor of her is the most addicting thing I've ever tasted. Starting slowly, I tease her and slowly build up pressure and speed.

As I lick and suck on her clit, she tenses up. When I insert two fingers into her and find the spot that makes her arch off the bed, she moans so perfectly that I want to remember the sound to get me off every time I want relief.

My hands move up to her breasts and massage them as I continue to tantalize her with my mouth. When she moans louder, I know she's getting close, so I focus on one spot that seems to make her go wild.

When she reaches the peak of orgasm, she cries out in pleasure. But I don't stop until every last cry and pulse has been taken from her body. After it's over, she is panting heavily, unable to move or speak for a few moments. Finally, she comes back down from the high.

I slowly pull away from her body, kissing the inside of each thigh before kneeling on the bed and unzipping my pants. Then I pull out my hard-as-steal cock. Reaching into my pocket, I take out the condom I'd put in there earlier and roll it on before settling back between her legs.

When she slides her legs up my back, wrapping them around me, and pulling me closer to her body, I take that as a sign of permission. Then I push in slowly, letting her get used to the size of me before going in deeper.

Each thrust is met with a moan from her lips and soon we are both lost in the pleasure of it all. I look into her eyes as our bodies move together and it's like nothing else I've ever experienced before.

We reach our peak together and come crashing down in a sweaty heap on the bed, both completely satisfied with our experience.

Collapsing beside her, it takes a moment to catch my breath. Then I undo the handcuffs and make sure she is covered and comfortable before getting up, disposing of the condom, and grabbing a bottle of water for her. I open it and hand it to her before climbing back into bed.

As I watch Gemma come down, I know she's in her head.

"Is this the part where I get up and leave?" she asks.

I smile at her innocence in all this. It's so damn cute but also proves she is much too good for me.

"This is the part where you let me hold you. It's called aftercare and sometimes doms need it as much or more than subs."

She nods and relaxes as I lie on my side, pulling her into me with her back to my chest. When I wrap an arm around her, she clasps it to her.

After we hold each other for a moment in a comfortable silence, I need to know what is on her mind. It's almost overpowering.

"Did you enjoy what we did?" I ask.

"Yes, very much so."

When she speaks, I can hear the smile in her voice. The last of the tension in me fades away with her words.

We had very little talk beforehand of how the night would go, and that just isn't like me.

"Good. I did too." I tell her, feeling the need to reassure her.

Turning into my arms, she faces me. Then she raises her hand and gently touches my cheek. I tense, as I don't let people touch me, and for good reason. But I don't let on. I just wait to see her next move.

When a brilliant smile crosses her face, I know right then I want to see her again.

"Will you come back tomorrow? I'll put your name on the list as my guest." Later, I will analyze my feelings. Right now I just wait for her answer.

Chapter 3
Gemma

When I search his eyes, it looks like he means it, that he wants me to come back. I sure as hell want to come back and spend another night with him. This was the most amazing night of my life and the best sex I've ever had. But there is something more between us. I can feel it.

"Yes, I'll come back," I say.

We spend a few more minutes cuddling before he helps me get dressed. He hadn't removed any of his clothes other than his suit jacket. I guess he was just so worked up that he didn't want to wait and that's kind of hot.

"I'll walk you to your car."

"Oh, you don't have to do that." I try to brush him off, but he stops in his tracks and turns to look at me.

"I will always make sure you get where you are going safely. Neither will I allow you to walk out into the parking lot at night in Chicago alone, no matter how safe Club Red's parking lot is."

Even though Skye boasted about how safe Club Red is, even the parking lot, I won't lie, having him there will put my already spinning mind at ease.

"Okay. Thank you."

He waits while I use the mirror to fix my hair. Not once did he rush me. Then, taking my hand, he walks me back downstairs and to the locker room.

"Go get your stuff. I will wait right here in the hall for you."

Making my way to the locker room, I take a deep breath. Finally able to since I'm away from him for just a moment. I can't believe I did that. Sex with a stranger is so not me. I don't do one-night stands, though if I'm seeing him again tomorrow, is it a one-night stand?

I guess if you are going to have sex with a stranger, this is the place to do it. Everyone is screened and clean, and it's about as safe as you can get it. Opening the locker, I get my stuff while wondering if Skye is still here or if she is already home. I guess I will find out soon.

Then I put my coat on, so I'm covered. This skimpy dress shows too much is not something that I would normally wear.

Taking some time to clear my head, I go out into the hall. Carter is waiting for me, just like he said he would be. Once again, he takes my hand, and I wonder if hand-holding means something more here than him just helping me out to my car.

Everyone in the lobby seems to know him. Even though they see us together, it's as if there is an understanding not to bother him. Once outside, he seems to relax slightly.

"Where is your car?" he asks.

"Umm over here. It's my friend Skye's car. She let me have the keys and she got a ride home with a friend." I walk in the direction we parked in, hitting the key fob button to see which car lights up because I can't remember which row we parked down.

He chuckles beside me as we head toward the car. He opens the door for me to get in.

"I had a really good time tonight," I tell him. Though I'm not sure how the night is supposed to end when you have sex with a stranger at a sex club.

"I did too, and I'll look forward to seeing you tomorrow night." He leans in, and kisses my cheek. Even that soft kiss sends tingles straight to my core.

Not knowing what to say, I smile, nod, and get in the car. Once I'm seated and my seatbelt is on, he closes the door behind me. When he steps to the side and watches me leave the parking lot, my heart races the entire time.

A final look in the rearview mirror before pulling onto the street and I can see he's still watching me. The whole way home, my brain tries to process what is going on. I want to call Summer and talk to her, but this seems a little weird even for our relationship. What would I say? 'Hey, I checked out the sex club you and my dad met at, and I met someone too.' Yeah, I think I'll talk to Skye.

When I got back to our apartment, thankfully, she was there and up.

"Okay, I stopped and got those cupcakes you love because I need details and it's totally a bribe. I know you were there and when I left, I saw the car was still there. SO?!"

"I promise details, but I want to shower and change first. Then let's open a bottle of wine, relax, and you have a deal," I say.

She lets out a squeal of excitement.

Rushing through my shower, partly not wanting to wash off Carter's scent, but also needing to wash tonight away. That way I can start over in the morning with a clear mind.

As the hot water cascades over my body, I think back to everything that happened. The way his hands felt on my body, the way he kissed me, and how he said he wanted to see me again tomorrow. I have no idea what that means or if this is just a one-night stand, but I guess I'll find out soon enough.

I step out of the shower, feeling more refreshed and ready for whatever comes next.

Once I am in my PJs, I go to the living room. Skye has moved the cupcakes to the coffee table along with a bottle of wine.

"So, what happened? I didn't see you with anyone, but I was distracted myself."

Not wasting any time, I tell her all the details of my night, from Carter walking up and our time in the main room to him taking me back to his room, on the third floor. Her eyes get huge when I mention the third floor, but she lets me tell the entire story.

"Wow. Good call on the wine," she says, refilling our glasses. "I don't know who has rooms on the third floor. I just know what I was told. But if he's up there, then he's a big deal at the club. How do you feel about what happened?"

"I honestly don't know. My mind is whirling, and I haven't had time to process it all."

"Well, don't make any decisions tonight. Get some sleep and we can chat in the morning and see where your head is. Whatever you decide, I will support you. I'll go back to the club with you or stay home and have a movie night in. It's your choice." She hugs me and we finish up the wine before heading to bed.

I don't remember falling asleep. I tossed and turned all night, but the smell of bacon, coffee, and French toast has me wide awake now. Getting up, I walk to the kitchen to find Skye making breakfast.

"How did you sleep?" She asks once I've had a bit of coffee.

"Like shit."

"I figured. Just for you, I made the coffee extra strong."

"I think I want to go back," I say, surprising even myself.

"By the look on your face, I'm guessing you hadn't made the decision until right now, huh?"

"Yeah, I dreamed about its last night, and I'm scared. Yet I think it's one of those things that I will always regret if I don't do it," I admit.

"Then you are doing the right thing."

We have breakfast and plan what I'm going to wear and what we are going to do to keep my mind off tonight. Since we both don't work today, we are thinking of going shopping. So after breakfast, we get ready to go.

Skye always takes longer than me to get ready, and as I'm waiting on her, there is a knock on the door. I open it to find a beautifully wrapped box on the ground in front of the door, but no one in sight.

The box is beautifully wrapped in shimmering gold paper, tied with velvet ribbon. I can barely make out my name scrawled in elegant calligraphy on the top. I carefully pick it up, feeling the weight of it in my hands, and take it inside.

"Oh, wow, what did you order?" Skye asks, joining me in the living room.

"Nothing. I wasn't expecting anything." I'm trying to rack my brain and figure out if I've ordered anything.

"Maybe you got in some late-night shopping you forgot about?" I shrug and open the box. Whatever is inside is wrapped in gold tissue paper and there is a note on top with my name beautifully scrawled on top.

Gemma,

I can't wait to see you tonight.

I thought you could use something to wear.

Wear this, and ONLY this.

Carter

The handwriting is masculine but neater than my own.

"Wow. Let's see what he picked out." Skye is almost giddy with excitement.

When I pull back the tissue paper, I find a tiny black dress.

Whatever the fabric of the dress is, it's the softest material I've ever touched in my life. Actually, it looks like it was tailor-made to fit me. It's a simple black dress, but eye-catching with a plunging neckline that borders on showing almost too much cleavage.

Skye is practically bouncing with excitement. "You have to try it on!" she exclaims. "I bet it'll look amazing on you."

I hesitate for only a moment with thoughts of how Carter got my address and his motives behind sending me the dress. If he had as much pull as Skye thinks he does, then he could have gotten it from the Club. Skye practically shoves me toward my room.

As the dress slips over me, I remember he said he wanted me to wear the dress and only the dress. Since the material forms to my skin, you would see a bra or panty outline easily. But to even get to Club Red, I'll have to wear a dress over it, so everything is covered. It's not something I'd normally wear out of the bedroom.

Opening my door, I show Skye.

When she sees me, her jaw drops. "Holy shit, you are going to have every guy in that place drooling over you! Please tell me you will let me do your hair and makeup!"

I agree hoping it will take my mind off things. With no need to go shopping now, we sit down to catch up on our TV shows, but they do nothing to calm my nerves about tonight.

Chapter 4
Carter

I sat at my desk and checked my email again, finally seeing that the package had been delivered to Gemma. Her name is so unique it wasn't hard to find her in the Club Red system.

Last night, I felt she was hesitant to agree to come back. If she had time to sleep on it, her mind might get the best of her, so I wanted to remind her I want her here tonight.

"Hey, they are waiting for us by the stage." Hunter peeks his head into my office.

Hunter is my partner and co-owner of Club Red. When I had the idea, he jumped on board feet first and took the risk with me. One that has paid out ten times over in the last few years. It set him and his son up, and that's all I ever wanted was to make sure they were taken care of.

Since we were in boot camp together, we have been best friends. There was no one else I'd have trusted to have my back and help me run the club than him. When Hunter became a single dad, I took on the responsibility to ensure they never went without, even though he stressed over and over that I didn't need to worry about them.

"All right, let's go get this over with." I stand up from my desk and button my suit jacket.

Then I follow him into the main room and to the tables in front of the stage where the other guys are gathered. These are the founding members and the ones with the most skin in the game when it comes to Club Red. They have private rooms on the third floor and a say in how the club is run.

In addition, they help bring in new people, and we'd be lost without them. They are also strategic members of the city government and often help us if any problems arise. Like today.

There is food on the tables, and drinks are already flowing. It's easier to chat when everyone is relaxed, and with some of the tempers in this room, we found that out the hard way.

"Who was that bombshell I saw you will last night?" Cade asks.

He's the youngest guy in the group and a tech genius. He created a social media website exclusively for kinky people and the BDSM community. It's been a way to promote Club Red and another stream of income for the club since we added the upgraded memberships.

"She is mine," I say, not liking the other guys having their eyes on her.

"Whoa, man, was just asking. Usually, you aren't with a sub without a contract, so I didn't know," Cade says.

I wince. He isn't wrong. I'm very formal with my arrangements. I don't do things like last night without it being planned out, but Gemma is different. How she's different, I just can't put it into words right now.

"Did you scene without a contract in place?" Gage asks.

Gage is a professor at a local college who has made good money with some discoveries he made at the university. He's crazy book-smart, has street smarts, and is not a bad guy to have on your team.

"I did, but this isn't why we are here."

All the guys start speaking at once, asking questions and talking to each other.

I look over with a plea for help at Hunter, who is sitting next to me.

He chuckles before leaning in to talk to me. "I'll help you out of this, but you will have to tell me everything later."

"Deal." If I'm going to tell anyone, I'd rather it be Hunter.

"Okay, guys, unless you want us to pry deep into your sub relationships, then we should drop this," Hunter says, and everyone grumbles.

"Maybe we should focus on why we are here?" Mase says, making everyone go silent.

Mase is by far our most powerful member. He's the head of a mafia family and is pretty much the muscle behind Club Red when needed. For a mafia guy, he's one of the better ones and seems to have a moral compass, which is why he was welcomed into our inner circle.

"Okay, we all know members and guests are vetted harshly here. Probably more so than other clubs in other cities, for obvious reasons," I say, looking over at Mase. "Sadly, we have had a leak."

"What kind of leak?" Ridge says.

Ridge was the first person Hunter and I brought into Club Red. We poached him from a smaller club because he is a great teacher for doms and is willing to work with new subs. He sets up a lot of lessons here at the club and is in charge of all the newbies. In theory, he should be where Gemma starts.

Like hell is Ridge getting his hands on my Gemma. Fuck, she isn't mine. I have to get her off my mind and focus right now.

"During the virgin auction we had a few months back," I say, and I'm interrupted by expletives flying around the room.

Due to popular demand, we had a virgin auction in the club. It was a great way to raise money for charity and was a tremendous success. Got a few new members out of it too.

"Time with a virgin. Be careful of your words, gentlemen," Troy says.

He's our in-house lawyer, club member, and attorney to many members as well.

"Well, either way, we need more than watching our words now," Hunter says.

"What exactly happened?" Sawyer asks.

He's an FBI agent and our eyes and ear about what is going on with law enforcement. A club like this is always on the radar because many don't understand what we do and are watching us for any sign of sex trade or sex work.

"Some photos were leaked from the event," I say

Hunter hands out photos he printed out earlier this morning once we saw the leak.

"We need to have security go over the video footage from that night and see if we can see who it is," Zander says.

He's another founding member and our head of security. With a military background specializing in security and intelligence, he's an asset to our team.

"I'd also like to bring in a few more guys. With this leak, I think we will need it. I'd like to reach out to Oakside and offer them the job first."

Oakside works with military men and women who are wounded in action. The staff at Oakside gets them the treatment they need. What's great about Oakside is they also help retired military transition into the civilian world, setting them up with jobs, school, housing, and more.

Zander has worked closely with them ever since they opened, and we have a few security guys from there.

"I agree. Let's do it. We'll want extra eyes on the cameras, especially at events, and more plainclothes men on the floor. But we don't want members to know we are upping security for any reason."

Everyone agrees. No need to raise an alarm and scare people away if we don't need to.

"Even with full transparency, there are always rumblings about Club Red and its members," Sawyers says as he looks over at Mase, who flips him off.

We all know Mase and his past. But we all have our reasons for being here, and as that song goes that the girls like to play here, 'If you go down, I'm going down too.' It's what holds this group together.

"But I've not heard any more rumors than normal," Sawyer finishes.

"That's because these photos haven't been released yet. They were sent to me and are going out sometime in the next forty-eight hours. I have tried all our usual methods, but I have been able to get them to agree to is to blur the girls' faces from the photos," Hunter says.

Mase is instantly on his phone. His fingers are flying across the screen, and we wait for him to say something.

"Let me see the file," he holds his hand out without taking his eyes off his phone. His tone is cold, and it's his *do as I say or else* tone that he uses in work mode.

Hunter hands it over, and Mase opens it, taking a few photos and sending them off.

"I've got a few guys on it. With any luck, we can stop them before they're printed... one way or another." He says, glancing at Sawyer.

We can all read between the lines. His methods may not be exactly legal, but when it comes to protecting us and the club, I don't think anyone here will complain.

"Since we are all here, there are a few small things you should know," I say, trying to break some of the tension in the room.

All eyes swing to me as I go over small items concerning the club.

"We are bringing in a marketing intern to help in the office. He's a friend of Cade's. His name is Kyle, and while he was fresh out of college when I talked to him, he was very professional, seemed intelligent, and had some great ideas."

"And you are going to let Seth train him?" Ridge asks with a sarcastic laugh.

Seth is our guy who runs the marketing office under Cade. He was great when we started, but things have started to slip, and he keeps mentioning how he wants to open his own club someday. The way he says it rubs me the wrong way.

Even though I can't say why, my gut doesn't like it. Troy, our lawyer, just keeps reminding me when he made the contract, he made sure to include a non-compete for all employees, and it's ironclad. That has to be enough for now.

"I'm going to be working with him," Cade says.

This whole thing was Cade's idea, after all. I think he sees a lot of himself in the kid and wants to help him out. Kyle is crazy smart, so it can't hurt to have him on our side in the years to come.

"Do we need some marketing kid, especially with everything going on?" Mase asks, and several heads around the table nod.

"Need? Probably not, but Kyle is one of the best hackers I've seen in years. Thankfully, he's used those skills for good. I think he's someone we will want on our team, especially with everything going on," Cade says.

"I agree with him on that. I wasn't thrilled to bring in a kid, either. I expected him to want to be here for the wrong reasons. Most kids his age think working here means free non-stop sex. Though he's mature beyond his age and really seems to be here for the job. I've checked out his socials, and it wasn't just an act," I tell them.

Their opinions are important, but, in the end, I have the final say in this. Right now, I just let them talk because now that everything is settled, the only thing on my mind is Gemma and how long before I can get my hands on her again.

Chapter 5
Gemma

"Ready to go?" Skye peeks her head into my room and asks. I've been standing in front of the mirror in the dress Carter bought for me for the last twenty minutes.

The dress is beautiful and fits me like a glove. I have no idea where he got it. It's short, skintight, and shows way more cleavage than I would ever choose on my own. I have no bra or underwear on, and I feel quite exposed.

Until we get to the club, I'm wearing a T-shirt dress over it. Then I grab a sweater and follow Skye out the door.

"You look hot in that dress. I can see why he picked it," Skye says once we are in the car.

"I guess. It's just not me. Am I doing the right thing going back tonight?"

"Don't start second-guessing yourself now. Feel things out. If you don't want to scene with him, just say red. You don't have to do anything you don't want to do. But don't back out now because of nerves," she says, reaching over and taking my hand.

She's right. If I back out, I know I'll regret it. But my anxiety is hitting me hard. Closing my eyes, I take a deep breath and think about last night and how great it felt, and how safe he made me feel.

Before I know it, we are at the Club, and the butterflies in my belly are in full force and have tripled since we left the apartment.

Skye practically drags me inside. At the receptionist's desk, she looks up and smiles. It's the same lady from last night.

"I'm so glad you are back, dear! Now Carter left you a pass on his account. Let me see the card you got last night, and I will link the two, and you will be good to go for as long as you are his," she says.

"I, well, I'm not..." I start to say.

"Perfect. I'll explain it all to her." Skye interrupts me and then keeps talking until the lady hands my card back, and Skye drags me to the locker room.

"What the hell?" I ask once we are alone.

"That is a normal term here. You are under his protection, and he is sponsoring you. Don't make issues by contradicting your dom."

"But he isn't."

"As long as you are with him, he is. Even if just for tonight."

As I put my stuff in the locker, I think I have a lot to learn.

"You can take the car again. I'll get a ride," Skye informs me.

I don't know who keeps giving her a ride, but I am thankful. So, I take the car keys and remove the dress I wore over the one Carter sent. Instantly, I feel naked in just the small thin dress and my shoes.

"Girl, you look hot!" Skye links her arm to mine and practically pushes me out into the main room.

My eyes immediately scan for Carter, but I don't see him. Is he up in his suite watching me from above? I glance up to where I think his room is, but Skye pulls my attention back to her.

"Let's get a drink, and then you can hang out at the bar until he finds you. I'll make sure the bartender keeps an eye on you." She steers me to the bar and sits me down.

When she orders our drinks, she leans over the bar and talks to the bartender. They both look my way, and the bartender nods his head before making our drinks.

"Okay, so hang here, and Jax there will keep an eye on you. He says he remembers you from last night and who you were with. Have fun. See you at home." Skye kisses my cheek and heads off toward the stairs to the second floor.

I need to remember to ask where she keeps going and what she does here.

Once Skye disappears upstairs, I only get two sips of my drink before Carter appears next to me from almost out of nowhere.

"I'm really glad you came. I was worried you wouldn't."

"I would have backed out if it weren't for my roommate pushing me," I tell him as I take him in.

He's wearing a suit again tonight, a slightly different one. This is a darker gray with a black tie that looks like it's made from the same material as my dress.

"Then I need to remember to thank her," he says, letting his eyes roam over me. The lust in them is undeniable.

"You look stunning." He says as his eyes land on mine again.

"Thank you. And thank you for the dress." I tell him.

He nods and then looks out over the crowd before looking back at me. "Can I touch you?"

I simply nod.

He holds his hand out, and I take it, putting my mostly unfished drink on the bar. Then I let him lead me toward the couch. Just like last night, he pulls me into his lap so my back is to his chest.

Since I don't have underwear on tonight, I keep my legs clamped tightly closed. Of course, that makes him chuckle.

"You can use your safe word at any time, and we stop. We can go up to my room and be alone. I may be asking you to submit to me, but you are ultimately the one with control," he whispers as he rubs the sides of my legs.

As I relax, he places each of my legs over his and then spreads me wide. My entire body heats, and I'm sure I'm as red as a tomato when people nearby look over at us.

"Hey Carter," a man walks up and makes eye contact with Carter, almost like I'm not there.

"Hello. Have you seen my girl here?" he asks.

Finally, the man's eyes shift to me. Only when he looks over at me do his eyes lock between my thighs.

"You can touch her if you want," Carter tells him, and the guy moves to his knees in front of me.

He looks up at Carter before running a finger over my slit.

When I gasp, the guy smirks.

"Your girl is wet," he tells Carter, but I'm not sure who he's trying to impress.

Carter doesn't say anything but runs his fingers through my hair and kisses me on the neck before nodding at the guy.

The guy slides two fingers inside me, and I moan, pushing back into Carter. Immediately, he stops what he's doing and looks up at Carter.

"You can keep going," Carter tells him.

The guy smiles before going back to work. Taking his time exploring every inch of me with his fingers, I pant and get even wetter. Finally, he slips them out and licks them clean before standing and looking at Carter again.

"She's amazing," he says before walking away.

I'm still in shock from what just happened when Carter glides his lips across my neck. His hands move up my body until they are cupping my breasts, and his thumbs are rubbing circles around my nipples.

When he moves one hand until it is between my legs and rubs me in slow circles, I moan out loud.

"You are wet," he whispers in my ear and then pulls his hand away as another guy walks up.

"Carter," the man says with barely a smile.

"Would you like to play with her?" Carter asks this man, who is wearing nothing but leather pants with his six-pack abs on full display.

It doesn't go unnoticed by me that he isn't using any of the guy's names or mine.

The guy nods, kneeling in front of me.

Carter moves his hands away from my body, and the guy takes over. He uses one hand to spread me open and then uses his fingers to stimulate my clitoris in a way I didn't know was possible.

His touch is gentle but firm, and he knows exactly how to move his fingers so that he brings me to an intense orgasm that makes my entire body shake.

He looks up at Carter with a satisfied smirk before standing up and walking away, leaving me dazed and breathless.

Carter picks me up and carries me to the elevator. When I look up at him, he doesn't look happy, and I start to wonder what I did wrong.

"Carter?" I ask once we are alone in the elevator, and he sets me down on shaky feet.

"He made you cum," he says, clearly angry. Then taking my hand, he leads me to his third-floor room.

"Wasn't that the point?" I ask, but he doesn't answer until we are in his room.

"I am the only one who makes you cum from this moment on. Do you understand?"

"Yes, sir," I say, liking the idea more than I should.

He moves and sits down on the couch.

"Good. Now come here," he orders.

I walk over to him and take the hand he is holding out to me.

Then he pulls me across his legs, bottoms up, and spanks me. I gasp at the sudden pain and then moan as he does it again and again. The pain is mixed with pleasure that builds inside of me until I can't take it anymore.

He stops the spanking and then slides his fingers between my legs, stroking me in a way that makes my body quiver with pleasure. He knows just where to touch me, to make me wetter and more aroused than ever before while pushing me closer and closer to the edge until I can't hold back anymore.

I scream out as wave after wave of pleasure washes over me, my body trembling from head to toe as I ride out the intense orgasm. When I finally come down from it, Carter pulls his hand away and helps me stand up straight before looking into my eyes.

"No one else will make you feel like that," he says in a voice filled with a possessiveness that makes my heart skip a beat.

"No one," I whisper back, knowing I would never want anyone else to make me feel the way Carter does.

He then reaches down and undoes his pants, pulls out his cock, and takes a condom from his pocket. After rolling on the condom, he takes my hand, pulling me in to straddle him.

Wrapping my legs around him, I sink onto his cock, gasping as he thrusts inside of me. He isn't being gentle, almost like he's still mad at me.

The sensation of him pushing inside me is like nothing I've ever felt before, and the more he thrusts, the more pleasure I feel. I wrap my arms around his neck just to hold on as he kisses my neck.

"No other man will know what it's like to have his cock inside you like this. Not while you are mine. No other man will feel you cum and squeeze him so perfectly," he whispers.

His words send shivers down my spine. I moan against his neck, pushing myself harder into him as he continues to thrust deep inside me.

He grabs ahold of my hips, pushing himself even deeper as he moves faster and faster. I can feel the pleasure building up inside me until I feel my pussy pulsing.

"Don't you dare cum," he growls.

I bite my lip, trying to hold back the orgasm begging to be released. Squeezing my eyes shut, I focus on breathing as Carter continues to thrust inside me, pushing me closer and closer to the edge.

"Good girl," he says.

He then reaches down between us, stroking my clit as he continues to move inside me. I gasp at the sensation, and Carter knows I'm about to cum. Finally, he presses his lips against mine, kissing me deeply as he whispers in my ear. "Cum for me."

I let out a loud moan as I reach my peak. Wave after wave of pleasure courses through my body until I collapse against him, completely spent.

The next thing I know, I'm wrapped up in his arms, sitting on his lap on the couch, under a black blanket, with my head on his shoulder. For the second time in a row, he barely removed his clothes. Maybe he just gets too into the moment.

"Do you want some water?" he asks.

Pulling me from my thoughts, I notice his voice is back to the soft Carter I met yesterday.

"Yes, please," I say. When he hands me a bottle, I drink about half of it as he watches me. The approval is clear on his face.

"You need to drink more water than normal the days you spend... here," he says as if he's choosing his words carefully.

I nod, not wanting to ask why.

After some more time cuddling in his lap, we finally fix our clothes.

"Did you enjoy tonight?" Carter asks as he studies my reaction.

"Yeah, I did. It's not something I'd normally do, but yeah, I liked it."

He nods and then walks over to his desk, opens a drawer, pulls out a folder, and walks over to me.

"This is a contract. Between you and me for us to keep meeting like this." He hands me the file, and I take it hesitantly.

"What's in the contract?" I ask without even opening it.

"Agreeing to be exclusive with me, NDA, limits, rules if you are to mine. Things like that."

"NDA? So, I can't talk about this with anyone?" My stomach churns, and I start to get the feeling I did when Brett Camden made me his secret girlfriend on the bus in sixth grade but denied it to anyone who asked.

"Your friend who brought you here and anyone in the club you can talk to. It's an NDA for people not at the club. We come here to protect ourselves, and many measures are being taken to keep our Club Red life separate from our everyday life." He isn't saying it, but I get it. He has to have money to be on the third floor. The suit tipped me off, too. He's probably some important businessman, and the last thing he needs is for this to get out.

"Okay," I say. The high I was on when in his arms is long gone.

"This means we are exclusive to each other in and out of Club Red. My limits are in there as well. Read it and take some time to think.

Next weekend we can meet back here. Saturday, if that works. I can answer any questions you might have," he says.

Is he trying to cheer me up? Putting on a smile, I gather my things. "That works," I say.

"Hey, Gemma?" He asks as I move toward the door.

I stop and turn back toward him. "Yes?"

"Can I get your number? Mine is in the contract in case you have any questions."

With that, I can't help but laugh. Though he just watches me.

"We did this all backward. Normally, the guy asks for the girl's number so he can try to get laid." I say. Still laughing, I take a pen and piece of paper off his desk, writing my name and number on it.

"While we have our kinks, I think you will find most guys here are better gentlemen than the guys outside this club."

"That is what Skye says, too," I say, handing him my number.

Once again, he walks me out to the car like last night. Honestly, I could get used to this. It's nice as a woman not to have to be on high alert in the city just to walk to my car.

"We will talk soon," Carter says, leaning in to kiss my cheek.

When I get home and check my phone, I have a text from an unknown number. Checking it against the contract, I see it's Carter, so I save it on my phone.

Carter: Let me know that you make it home safe.

Me: I'm home.

Carter: Sweet dreams, baby girl. Dream of me.

Chapter 6

Agent X

I'm used to having my phone waking me up, but it's normally with work calls. Not because the search alerts I have set up keep going off.

Something big is happening.

Sitting up, I stretch and then check my phone. It's my Club Red alert. I try not to get too excited. Normally the alerts on the club are nothing, maybe mentions on social media or write-ups on some small blog.

So, I check the headlines.

Virgin Auction Held at Club Red

Club Red Selling Off Virgins? Here is what we know!

Need a quick way to make some money? Sell that V-Card at Club Red, baby!

What the hell?

I've been tracking Club Red for years. Years. And nothing like this has even been hinted at. They have been so squeaky clean; it's been annoying.

Jumping out of bed, I rush to my office, pulling out my boxes of Club Red research.

Research that has led me nowhere until today. Then I get on my computer and start reading the articles. There are a few photos of women on stage, their faces blurred, and men in the audience. There is no way to prove it's a virgin auction from the photos, and I know that. But the key will be from where the photos came from and who is willing to speak about them.

So, I start making phone calls. The first one is to my boss.

"Hey, I have a lead on a case. I am making a few calls and have a few stops before I'm in the office."

"This better be good." He grumbles before hanging up the phone.

Wasting no time, I call up my contacts. I need to get details on where this information is coming from. But no one's willing to reveal their source. Not that I can blame them. But what I do find out is that it was from someone that was there that night who took the pictures and leaked the information.

No one will confirm anything more than that, which leaves me with a bunch of questions. Is it a disgruntled member? Was it a guest of someone that was there that night? Judging by the photos, I doubt it was one of the girls that were up on stage.

There's also the question of why leak it secretly. If it was a disgruntled member, you would assume they'd go right to the cops and get the place shut down or maybe hold it as blackmail against the owners. They wouldn't expose the girls to the public, especially if the girls are innocent.

Were the girls forced into this auction? This then opens up a whole new door to questions like where did they come from. How long has the club been into these kinds of practices? All of which I can't get answers to from any of my contacts.

For years, I've been gathering information on Club Red. Something about the club and its practices never sat right with me, yet I've never had enough evidence to do anything about it.

There is no police involvement. As much as I wish they would open an investigation, it could cost millions of dollars on someone's hunch.

I pack up the file I have on Club Red, add the new information to it and get ready for work. I've got a few stops to make on my way in.

My first stop was at the local liquor store to buy a large bottle of Southern Comfort. My second stop is the grocery store. Then I drive down the Dan Ryan Expressway to the side of town that many seemed to turn a blind eye to.

Many of the homeless live under the overpasses here. I'm looking for one person in particular. He's not very friendly unless you know exactly how to work him for the information that you need. But I've discovered he's the gossip amongst the homeless crew in Chicago. If something's going on, he's going to know.

"Hey, Striker, how have you been?" I ask, walking up to him as he's eyeing the bags in my hands.

"Just trying to survive, man."

"Well, I'm hoping to make that a bit easier with a mutually beneficial exchange."

He knows I want information. Whether he's willing to give it to me or not will depend on if he likes my offerings.

"Well, let's see what you got."

I start with the bag from the grocery store. Pulling out several of his favorite snacks, a rotisserie chicken, protein bars, and a granola trail mix. All of which he can keep or would be great for trade if he goes that route.

"I'm looking for information on this virgin auction that happened at Club Red." I hand the bag to him.

"Yeah, I heard about it. Since last night, it's been all over the place." He says, picking through the bags before turning and setting them with his other belongings.

"Any idea where the pictures may have come from?" I ask. Then I hold up the bottle of Southern Comfort.

"Word on the street is that they came from someone in the club who has an ulterior motive."

"Any idea who or what the motive is?"

"Nah, no one knows. It's been top secret, but I can tell you that you're not the only one who wants to find out. There have been some pretty big rewards put out for any information that leads to the capture of whoever leaked the photos."

"How big of a reward?"

"Life-changing, man. One million dollars." He takes the Southern Comfort from me, holding on to it like I might try to snatch it back.

"Any info on the actual virgin auction? Where did the women come from?" I ask, reaching into my pocket. Then pull out a one hundred dollar bill.

"They were all willing. Most of the money from the auction went right into the grils' pockets. Though, it wasn't called a virgin auction. That's all the information I got, man." He takes the money from me, and I know he's telling the truth because he knows I would be offering more money if he had more information. Money is something that he won't turn down because it buys the one thing I won't supply him with: drugs.

Thanking him for his time, I head out.

On my drive to work, there's one thing I can't seem to get out of my mind. Who in the hell would pay one million for information on the people who leaked the photos?

Is there someone else with much deeper pockets working on this case? Or is it someone trying to protect Club Red?

Once at work, I grab my folder and go right into my boss's office.

"Alright, let's hear it," he says without even looking up from his phone.

"So, there was a huge expose on Club Red today. Photos leaked from a virgin auction they held. This club has been on my radar for a few years. There hasn't been enough to do anything with or even waste your time on, but I've been collecting information over the years."

"Go on." He sets his phone down and gives me his attention, which is a good sign.

"Club Red is a sex club, which, while not illegal, skirts the law in many areas. No one has ever come out directly to speak against the club. But the rumors that float around are what have caught my attention and made me keep an eye on them."

"What kind of rumors?"

"Rumors those women can't leave once they're there. That they're abused, and these men hit them. Some women are kept in cages or on a leash."

"But you can't prove any of this?" my boss asks.

"No. These photos are the first leak of anything inside the club. Membership is strict, and you have to know someone who knows someone to get in. There's also been some mafia activity near the club, but I haven't been able to link any of the families to the club as of yet."

As I continue, my boss looks over the reports, articles, and photos that were released today.

"I went and talked to one of my informants, and there's news on Club Red. Someone wants to know who is behind this leak badly enough they're offering a million-dollar reward. The streets have heard about Club Red as well and this virgin auction. Only it wasn't called a virgin auction when it happened."

"So, this could have been any event, and someone snagged the picture and made up some story to go with it. Without any proof, we can't do anything or even put any man-hours into this. You are free to keep investigating on your own time. If you find anything, let me know."

I had a feeling this would be his answer. While I know in my heart there is not enough to go on, the fact that he's allowing me to keep using my free time on it and not telling me to drop it all together gives me hope.

"Do I have your permission to use office computers and maybe talk to some other people and see if they've heard anything?"

He pauses and looks at me. "Yes, but again only on your own time, and don't harass any of my men."

"You have my word."

As I'm leaving the room, he stops me one more time.

"Keep me updated on what you find out."

It's not much, but this might be what I need to finally, after all these years, take Club Red down.

Chapter 7
Carter

Me: Good Morning, Beautiful.

As I was getting ready for work this morning, I stared at the text I sent Gemma. It's become a habit to text her every morning. It seems to open her up to chat with me throughout the day.

I like getting her text messages more than I should. Over this last week, she has been reading the contract, or at least thinking about it, because she has been asking questions, which means she is taking this seriously.

All that said, she is normally up and texting me by now. So, going into this meeting with Hunter, Zander, and Sawyer, I'm more on edge than normal.

Tomorrow, I get to see her and get my hands on her again. A little release will do wonders for my tension with everything going on with Club Red right now.

When I walk into the meeting room here at Club Red, Zander and Sawyer are already there. The tension in the room is so thick you could cut it with a knife.

"Well, this can't be good," I whisper to Hunter, who nods in agreement as we take our seats.

Sawyer called this meeting with Hunter and me. We have asked Zander to hold more of these meetings because he works with the staff and has been taking on more duties around the club. Hunter and I have been thinking about pulling back some.

We have busted out butts to get the club up and going and always wanted to sit back and let it run. Just as we think we can do that, here comes trouble. Never fails.

"Out with it. I'm sure my imagination is worse than the actual truth," I say once we are all seated.

"Law enforcement and the Feds both have rumblings concerning Club Red and this virgin auction story. It's something that has caught their attention," Sawyer says.

"Caught their attention how?" Hunter asks.

"There's a guy in my office asking questions. Though when I talk with my boss, there's no formal investigation. So essentially, Club Red is now on their radar. Mostly because they want to make sure that the girls were up on the stage willingly and not forced."

"To prove that, we'd have to release names of the women for them to talk to, which would violate the contract we signed with them. Or law enforcement would have to get a warrant for that information," I say.

"Which they won't since it's not a formal investigation. Right now, they're just talking to people, seeing what comes up. Though I will say, it doesn't help that the informant sector seems to be hearing that there's a million-dollar reward for information on the people leaking the photos," Sawyer says.

"That has to be Mase, trying to bring people in with information," Zander says, and I know he's right.

"Well, he's not the only one searching for information. According to my sources, several cops have been sniffing around for information, too. My guess is they think if they can break this case, it would be leverage for a promotion."

"Who's asking questions?" I ask.

Sawyer just looks at me and doesn't say anything. He may be loyal to Club Red, but he's also loyal to those he works with too. Maybe more so because his loyalty to Club Red is more to protect himself.

"I feel like maybe we should have Troy here," Hunter says, reading my mind.

"Yeah, I already called him and filled him in. He should be here anytime now as he was wrapping up court this morning," Sawyer says.

With timing that can only be planned so well in the movies, the door to the meeting room opens, and in walks Troy.

"If I didn't have more meetings this afternoon, I would have poured myself a damn whiskey," he says, sitting down at the conference table.

"I completely understand. You could not pay me enough to do your job," I tell him, and I'm greeted with a bunch of nods across the room.

"So, what do we need to do to protect ourselves at this point?" I ask.

"Are there any updates since we talked?" Troy looks over at Sawyer, who shakes his head.

"Okay, in all honesty, rumblings happen all the time. If we can find a way to publicly discredit the source or the photos, that would be our best bet. Internally, we need to figure out who the hell leaked the photos, and they need to be dealt with sooner rather than later before there's another one. And off the record, you guys need to get rid of anything that uses the word virgin in the auction, and I mean burn it. Even though I know that we were careful with our wording with this, I also know some stuff slipped through in our planning sessions and in the office. Now's the time to take care of it.

And it needs to be one of you two. Don't pass that off to someone." Troy says, looking right at Hunter and me.

"Looks like we're in for a long night," Hunter says, shaking his head.

Just then, my phone goes off, and I try to fight the smile that wants to cross my face because I know that's Gemma based on the special notification sound I assigned her. So, pulling out my phone, I check to see what she had to say.

Gemma: Good morning. Skye had an early class today, and since I didn't have to work, I slept in longer than I thought I would.

Me: Well, get your rest while you can. You're going to need it this weekend. What are your plans for today?

Gemma: I'm going to go have lunch with my dad and my best friend. I keep waiting for each get-together for them to tell me she's pregnant. Maybe this is it.

Me: What am I missing here?

Gemma: Oh! A few months ago, my dad married my best friend, so she's now technically my stepmother. It was weird at first, but they're happy together, and that's all I ever wanted for my dad and her.

Me: Enjoy your lunch.

Gemma: What are your plans for today?

Me: Once I finish up this meeting, I have some office work to do. And then more meetings.

Gemma: Well, I hope they're all good meetings.

Somebody clears their throat loudly, and I look up, and every set of eyes in the room is on me.

"What?" I ask, setting my phone down.

"You're grinning like a damn fool. Who are you talking to?" Hunter asks.

"We have more important things to focus on than who I'm talking to," I try to redirect the meeting.

"It's the girl from last weekend, isn't it?" Zander asks. Now I know there's no hope of getting this meeting back on track until I answer a few questions.

"Yes, it is. We've been talking, and before anyone asks yes, I gave her a contract. She's been reviewing it this week and asking questions about it. That sort of thing," I tell them.

"I've known you for years, and I've seen you with several other subs, but you've never smiled like that when any of them messaged you," Hunter says.

While I know he's right, I'm not going to have this conversation. Besides, what the hell would I say? All I have is the cheesy stuff that I've never felt this way with another sub. Their exact reactions would be, *well, if you got laid more often, you wouldn't be having feelings like this.* So I go for the easier answer.

"She's new to the lifestyle, and yes, it's true. In the past, I usually avoided newbies. But I find I like guiding her and answering her questions more than I thought it would."

"Good for you. I always found the training to be very rewarding, and I hope you do too," Hunter says.

The other men agree, and finally, we get back to our meeting. Though as they talk and make plans, my mind is stuck on Gemma.

She is new to all this and will need more training than I can give her. I'm sure her friend is helping her, but if I'm going to keep her around, I need to make sure that I do this right. Also, I want to protect her from whatever comes of these rumors.

Chapter 8

Gemma

Once again, I'm looking over the contract Carter gave me. I haven't talked it over with Skye because she's been busy with work and school. Even though she graduated this summer, she went on for some advanced degree and had been working her butt off.

So, I haven't bothered her with this. I kept it to myself for now, and thankfully Carter has wanted to answer any questions I've had. Whatever I have not asked him, I've searched online for.

Earlier this week, Carter recommended I join this kinky social media site that Club Red hosts. People from all over the world can get on, talk, ask questions, find partners, etc. When I signed up, he put me under his protection on the website. I guess it's to keep the creeps away, but I've enjoyed reading many of the discussions going on.

Realizing I need to get going if I'm going to have lunch with my dad and Summer, I put the contract away and go to their house. It's still weird thinking of it as their house because it is the house I grew up in. A lot of things have changed since my dad married my best friend, but much has stayed the same too.

Often, the three of us would have lunches and dinners. We'd go out and do things because Summer was always welcome, and she spent more time at my house than she did her own. Both have sworn to me that nothing happened between them until they ran into each other at Club Red while I was out of town with my now ex-fiancé.

Though with how happy they are, I don't think I would have cared if it had. I hope to find someone and have as happy of a relationship as they do.

When I get to the house, I hesitate at the door. Normally I'd walk in without knocking, but now I'm worried about what I might walk in on. They know I'm coming over, so should I just go in?

Instead, I decide to knock, and it takes a minute before my dad answers the door. When he sees me on the other side, he looks utterly confused.

"Why are you knocking?" He asks as we head inside and back towards the kitchen.

"Because I don't want to walk in on something I don't want to see," I say honestly. Then I go over and hug Summer, whose cheeks flush when I mention walking in on something.

"If we know you're coming, I promise you're not going to walk in on something. Now, if you're coming over unexpectedly, just make your presence known. But you don't have to knock. This is still your house," My dad says, with Summer agreeing.

"If you say so. Do I have time to steal Summer away for some girl talk?"

"Yep, lunch will be ready in about twenty minutes," Dad says.

"Can we go talk out by the pool? The weather is beautiful, and I want to enjoy it," Summer says. Then she takes my hand and pulls me outside.

I know my dad is watching over Summer, but I know he can't hear us either.

"Okay, spill," Summer says as we sit on one of the lounge chairs that face the kitchen window.

"So, Skye dragged me to Club Red, and I met someone kind of," I start, and Summer jumps up and turns to face me.

"Oh, my God! That's awesome. Gemma, tell me everything."

She has a beaming smile on her face, and I love the type of energy that she gives. Summer has always been that friend to pump you up and encourage you to do things, and I guess maybe that's what I need right now.

"Well, he's older. Maybe not quite as old as my dad, but older than me."

"Older is better. It means more experience and less drama."

She's not wrong. The last thing I need is more drama.

"We've done stuff at the club that I never in a million years would have tried outside the club."

"That's kind of the point." I know she's right. It's pretty much the entire reason the club exists. How many of these people would explore their kinks outside of the club? Probably very few of them because the club is a safe haven.

"So, what's holding you up?" She asks because she's always been able to read me pretty well.

"He gave me a contract that he wants me to sign so that we can keep having fun at the club," I told her.

"Ah. The relationships in and out of the club are very different from what we're used to. Many of the people there, men and women, are at the top of their careers. They're important people in their everyday lives, and the last thing they want is for what they do at Club Red to get out. It's the whole reason they go to the club."

"I know that." Skye has told me the same thing.

"So, when these said individuals want something more permanent from someone, the contracts are the way to safeguard both them and you."

I look at her for a moment and then ask a question and brace myself for the answer.

"Did you and Dad have a contract after you met at Club Red?"

"No, but we knew each other, and we trusted each other. You don't know this man outside of Club Red, do you?"

"No, I don't."

"Then it stands to reason he wants to protect himself. What's in the contract?"

"His hard limits and my hard limits. We're to both get tested, and I'm to be on birth control because he doesn't want to use condoms. There is an exclusivity clause and an NDA. It states that he doesn't want a relationship outside Club Red. No dinner dates, that sort of thing."

"You're not allowed to talk about what happens?" She asks with the same hesitancy I had.

"I'm not allowed to talk to anyone who's not a member of Club Red. Basically, what happens stays within the club walls."

"That's reasonable. There are plenty of people inside the club you can go to with questions or concerns. Plus, it means you can still talk to me, Skye, and if you need to, even your dad."

"There is no way I'm talking to my dad about this, and I'd appreciate it if you don't mention it to him, either."

"He is going to ask me what we talked about."

"You can tell him that Skye dragged me to Club Red, and I was talking to you about it. That's it. I'm invoking the best friend clause here."

"Alright, let's go have lunch. Then you better have another topic to talk to your dad about because he's going to ask what we were talking about. Oh, one more thing. Are you going to sign the contract? Are you going to go back?"

"That's two things, Summer. I don't know about the contract just yet. But yes, I'm supposed to meet him tomorrow night. And yes, I plan on going."

"Good. Call me and let me know what happens. I don't care what time."

"I promise I will."

Giving her a big hug, we go inside for lunch. I just pray that we can avoid the topic of Club Red in front of my dad.

Right now, I'm standing in front of Club Red alone. I have the contract in one hand, but it's completely unsigned, and I'm not sure if I'm going to sign it yet. What I do know is I want to see how things go with Carter tonight.

He's been texting me every day, and he remembers the small things like checking how lunch went with my dad and Summer. It's nice to have someone so attentive to what I say. But that alone is not a reason to sign this contract. I was hoping to be able to talk to Skye about it, but we keep missing each other.

Leaving the contract in my locker, I take a deep breath and go out to the main room to find Carter.

When I walk in, I find him standing by the bar. As I walk over, he smiles at me and then leans back to say something to the bartender before turning his full attention to me.

"Right on time, I like that," he says, smiling.

Then the bartender hands him a glass, which he turns and gives to me.

Once again, proving he's been paying attention to what I've been drinking. Even though I don't drink much, I take a small sip, just enough to steady my nerves. But I like not knowing what he has in store for me.

"I had plans to talk to you about the contract tonight. But it's been a long and stressful week, and I've been looking forward to playing with you. If that's okay?"

I can hear the strain in his voice. While I am nervous, tonight must be about his needs too.

"That's fine with me," I say, taking another sip of my drink.

"Can I touch you?" he asks.

I nod.

When he takes my hand in his, we stand there for a moment as I take another sip of my drink before setting it on the bar. He finishes his and then takes me over to the couch.

"Do you remember my rule from last time?" he asks.

"You're the only one that makes me cum."

"Good girl. Don't break my rule."

Just like every night before, he sits me on his lap again with my back to his chest and my legs over his so he can spread them apart. I'm wearing the black dress he bought me and nothing else under it, as he had asked.

He rubs his hands up and down my arms before gripping my hips. Then he spread my legs wide, and once again, anyone walking by could see me on full display.

A man walks up that I haven't seen before, but Carter seems to know him. He's respectful and keeps eye contact with Carter.

"Your sub is beautiful," the man says.

"She is, and she listens so sweetly. She tastes just as sweet. Would you like a taste?" Carter asks, lifting the hem of my dress. Only then do the man's eyes land between my thighs.

"Yes, I would," the man says.

"Go ahead."

The man gets on his knees in front of me, looks me in the eye for just a moment, and smiles. Then his head dips down, and I feel his tongue on my clit.

"Fuck!" I exclaim, throwing my head back onto Carter's shoulder.

"Language," Carter chuckles and pinches my thigh.

Carter's hands run up my sides to the top of the dress. Then he pushes the straps down my shoulders and pulls my breasts out. All while the man in front of me runs his tongue over my clit again and again.

"Look at her tits. Aren't they perfect?" Carter asks.

The man stops to look up at me.

"Most beautiful pair I've ever seen. You are a lucky man." The man says before diving back to sucking on my clit.

Chapter 9
Gemma

An orgasm starts to creep its way in, and I try to push it down.

"You can do it. Control it." Carter whispers in my ear because, of course, he knows what this man is doing to me.

Squeezing my eyes shut, I think of the time I had to rush my dad to the ER because he sliced his hand open trying to fix the lawn mower.

"Thank you," Carter says to the guy, who stops but looks very reluctant to step away, though he does.

"Thank you for the taste." The man says to Carter and doesn't even look my way again.

I'm just starting to come down from that high when another man kneels in front of me.

"I'd be honored to have a taste," he says.

"Go ahead," Carter says.

This man runs his hands up my thighs and grips my hips before diving in for his taste. Instead of just licking like the last guy, he's running circles around my clit with his tongue. The orgasm I thought was fading is right back at the surface, wanting to break through again.

He licks and sucks on my clit in a way that has me arching my back and gripping the edge of the couch. All while Carter's hands move up and down my body cupping my breasts. With all the stimulation, I'm on a hair trigger.

The man stops licking me but keeps his mouth on my clit as he looks up at me with a mischievous grin. He then starts to hum against it, sending vibrations through my body that have me shaking and screaming out Carter's name.

"No, no, no. You can do it. Control it." Carter says as he grips my hips tightly.

At Carter's words, the man stops and looks up at me with a smile before getting back to work.

Taking deep breaths in and out, I focus on the music playing in the background until I feel like I can take control again.

After what feels like forever, the man stands up. I let out a sigh of relief, knowing that I made it without breaking Carter's rule.

"Good job, baby girl. You make me so proud," Carter says as he lightly kisses my neck.

When I take a deep breath and try to sit up, Carter keeps me pinned in place.

"I didn't say you should move."

"Go ahead," he says to a man I didn't see standing off to the side.

"No, wait..." I start, and everyone stops.

"What color?" Carter asks in a serious tone.

"Green, but..."

"Okay then, do as I say, baby girl."

The guy with bleached blonde hair kneels in front of me and traces the outline of my clit with his tongue.

He circles, licks, and then sucks it all while Carter's hands glide across my body, sending shivers up my spine.

The man moves from my clit to licking around my inner thighs and then back up again. He stops for a moment to look up at me before torturing me some more.

Carter runs his hands through my hair as he watches the man work, occasionally whispering encouragement or directions into my ear.

The seconds seem like hours before the man finally stands and is quickly replaced by the next one.

"This is the last one. I know you can do this," Carter whispers.

This man is different. He takes his time and explores my body with his hand as his tongue explores all on its own. He licks and sucks on my clit in a way that has me gripping the couch and wanting to give in to the orgasm.

But I manage to keep control, and when he's done, I'm left panting and shaking.

Carter pulls me up into his arms and holds me tight.

"You did it, baby girl," he whispers. "Now you can cum."

Before I've had time to catch my breath, Carter tossed me on the couch and moved between my legs. When he starts licking and sucking on my clit, I can't stop the moaning.

Since I've been on edge for what seems forever, it takes very little from Carter before waves of pleasure shoot through my body. I grip the couch as the orgasm builds until it finally breaks free.

The pleasure is intense and overwhelming, sending shockwaves of ecstasy through my body before finally subsiding.

I lay there panting and exhausted but feeling incredible. Carter pulls me close and kisses me gently before whispering in my ear.

"That was amazing, baby girl," he says, smiling. "You have no idea how proud I am of you."

Because I don't even have the energy to formulate words, I just smile.

Carter wraps me in a black blanket with the Club Red logo on it and picks me up, carrying me to the elevator and to his private room.

Finally, he sets me down on the couch and holds me. After a while, he gets me some water, which I drink and hand back to him.

"How do you feel?" He's stroking my hair in a way that makes me want to fall asleep right where I am.

"I'm good," I say drowsily.

"Excellent. You were so beautiful out there." He kisses my temple, asking, "How do you feel about what happened?"

"Well, I've never done anything like that before, but I've also never come so hard in my life," I tell him honestly.

"That's what I like to hear," he says with a smile.

"Have you had a chance to make up your mind on the contract?" he asks.

Immediately a wall goes back up that wasn't there a moment ago.

"I've gone over it and have been thinking about it."

"What are your thoughts and concerns?"

"Well, I like the idea of it being exclusive and to keep doing this. I'm honestly not sure where all my limits are, but I know a few of them."

"I'm open to exploring the other ones together. Just put down what you know you don't want, and we can go from there," he says.

"If I sign the contract, would you still be sharing me?"

"Do you want me to?"

"Yes," I tell him again, being honest. Because complete honesty and transparency are something he asks for in the contract.

"Then yes, once the contract is signed, I will be."

"Will we have sex out in the open room downstairs?"

"It's not something I normally do, but yes, we could," he says. But his eyes search my face, looking for something I'm not sure of.

"And if I signed it, you wouldn't be with anyone else?"

"No, not for as long as the contract is active. Neither of us would be with anyone else unless I opt to share you with someone else or you choose to share me with someone. However, that's something that would be discussed ahead of time."

I sit up and nod, wondering if I have any other questions.

Removing the blanket, he guides me to my knees on the floor between his legs. Then he unbuckles his pants, pulling his cock out.

He's hard, and as he strokes himself, I get my first good look at him. Damn, is his cock gorgeous, thick, and veiny.

With one hand, he cups the back of my head, guiding my mouth to the head of his cock.

I start licking and sucking him slowly and then faster as he moans in pleasure. As I run my tongue up and down his shaft, he talks dirty to me, telling me what a good girl I am for obeying his commands.

"That's it, baby girl. Just like that," he says in a low voice. When he thrusts his hips further into my mouth, I take him deeper.

"Fuck, your mouth feels like heaven," he moans.

His skin tastes salty and sweet, like a mix of honey and sea salt. His moans of pleasure echo through the room as he thrusts his hips further into my mouth.

When his breathing gets heavier, I know he's getting close, so I increase the suction on his cock while swirling my tongue around it.

"Oh God, I'm going to cum!"

He grips my hair as an orgasm rips through him. His cum spills into my mouth, making me moan, knowing I gave him this pleasure.

When he finally pulls out, I lick my lips clean before standing and fixing my dress. After straightening his clothes, he stands and pulls me into his arms.

Resting my head on his chest, we stand there holding each other until he speaks. "Look the contract over and think about it."

Then, moving away, he takes what looks like a business card from his pocket. "If you decide to sign it, then meet me at the address on this card Tuesday night. If you don't show, I promise I won't bother you again."

Without another word, he pulls me into a passionate kiss.

It's a kiss filled with a promise of something more than just the contract. His lips are gentle but insistent. His tongue explores my mouth with a hunger I've never felt before. When he pulls me closer, I can feel the heat radiating off his body as our tongues intertwine in a dance of sweet bliss.

While the kiss is slow, like we have all the time in the world, it's also erotic and steamy. I could stay like this forever. His hands move slowly down my back before cupping my ass, pulling me even closer to him.

I'm lost in the moment, feeling his warmth and passion surround me until finally, he steps back, breaking off the kiss and leaving me wanting more.

Like every night that we meet up at the club, he walks me down to the locker room and waits for me to gather my stuff. He eyes the folder with the contract but says nothing as he walks me out to my car.

Before I can say anything, he pulls me into another passionate kiss that leaves me breathless. When we finally move apart, he looks me in the eyes.

"Think about the contract," he says again. "And if you decide to sign it, meet me Tuesday night at the address on the card."

Nodding my head, I start the car.

As I drive away, I can feel his eyes on me until I exit the parking lot. The contract seems important to him, and now I have a deadline.

I have three days to sign it or never see him again.

Chapter 10
Carter

I'm sitting in my office in Club Red, getting nothing done as I stare at my phone. It's been one of the hardest things to do not to text Gemma since I saw her on Saturday. I don't want her to feel like I'm forcing her one way or another with the contract. It needs to be completely her decision.

Tomorrow night, the wait will be over. Either she will meet me or she won't. Part of me wants to call her and demand to know if she's going to sign the contract. I've never been this on edge about anyone possibly saying no before.

"Hey, you wanted me to let you know when that new guy was doing security," Hunter says, poking his head in.

Happy for the distraction, I thank him. We picked up a few new security guys, all from Oakside and all prior military. But this guy was former intelligence who had a top-secret security clearance. His eyes are sharp, and he has an eye like we've never seen. He's caught things around here that the average person would miss.

In one of his deployments, he lost both his legs in a bombing, so he's in a wheelchair, though he's going through rehab to learn to walk on prosthetics. He's the perfect candidate to sit in the security room and watch the cameras. Already he has caught someone stealing drinks after being told no more from the bar. It could have turned into a possibly dangerous situation. We have a drink minimum here for a reason.

When he caught one of our cleaning people taking a few shortcuts that I wasn't happy with, I asked Hunter to remind me the next time he was in. I want to say thank you to him personally.

Heading down to the security room, I find him getting set up for the night. Since the club hasn't opened yet, he's testing all the equipment to make sure everything is functioning properly.

"Hey, Hunter, before we go in there, I have an idea." I stop him in the hallway.

"What's up?"

Checking to make sure we're alone, I end up deciding to err on the side of caution. Since we're next to Hunter's office, we duck in there.

"If this guy is as good as you say he is about catching things, and if he continues to prove loyal, we should have him watch the footage from the night of the auction. Maybe he can catch something that we've missed."

I've watched the footage, and so have several of the other founding members, including Sawyer, Hunter, and Zander. We don't see anyone outright taking pictures, but we have some suspicious activity. Unfortunately, we can't act on suspicious activity alone.

"Yeah, I was thinking the same thing. But we need more time to see how he does and to make sure he's going to stick around before we show our hands on an event like that."

"I agree, but let's just keep it in mind as we work with him. All right, let's go to the security room,' I say.

"Paul, this is Carter, the other owner I was telling you about," Hunter says.

"Hey man, it's nice to meet you. Hunter told me a lot about you," he says.

Then he shakes my hand with a nice firm handshake, which is about all I need to know. Of course, I wouldn't expect anything else from a military man.

"How's the equipment?" I knew about the camera he was working on when we came in.

"It's in top-notch working order. Usually, when I come into a place, I expect to find at least something to fix. But so far, everything is fine here."

The shock in his voice is as clear as day.

"We pride ourselves on the safety of our members. So anytime something's broken, we waste no time fixing it. If any of our equipment is down even a few minutes that puts people in danger and at risk. Even though we have eyes on the ground," I say.

"I completely understand. While I know I still have a lot to learn, that's one thing that's been drilled into me since I've been here. Then again, in a place like this, I'd be worried if you didn't take safety seriously."

"Exactly. I just wanted to pop in so that you could put a face to the name and let you know that you can always come to me if any issues arise. Hunter here should have given you my phone number. You can call me anytime day or night. This club is our baby and we take it seriously. Remember, if there's a problem don't ever think that you're bothering us," I say. Then I shake his hand again before leaving.

Hunter follows me back to my office, closing and locking the door behind him.

"So, I saw you here with Gemma the other night," he says, walking over and pouring himself a drink.

"How do you know her?" With her being new, I figured not many people would know her name.

"I know her roommate, Skye. They come in together, so I asked." He shrugs his shoulders like it's nothing.

"And?" I ask, wanting him to get to the point of whatever this conversation is about.

"Did you sign a contract with her?" he asks, bringing me a glass of whiskey.

"She has a contract, but she hasn't signed it yet."

"Wow, she has you off of your game. I've not known you to play with a woman without the contract signed first. And you never play in the main space like that."

"She likes it." That's all I say, but he's right, I'm normally pretty private and don't play out in the open. But Gemma gets off on it and because she wants it, it makes me want it too.

Hunter stands, not taking any more of his drink.

"You know her dad's a member here, right?" he asks.

I freeze. I don't think we've ever had an issue like this before where a club member's child is also at the club.

"Who's her dad?"

"Knox Gentry. And before you ask, yes, according to Skye, he knows about her being here. Since he's now married, they only come to play for certain events and they worked it out so that they will not be here at the same time. But I've already put a flag on both of their accounts, so if one of them is checked in and the other shows up, the receptionist will let them know."

"Thank you," I say. Grateful that he's putting out a fire before I even realized there was one.

"Are you going to make her sign the contract?" he asks, finishing off his drink.

"I told her that if she's going to sign the contract, to meet me tomorrow night. If not, then I wouldn't bother her again."

"That explains why you're so on edge tonight. You should go home before you start scaring any of the staff." Hunter says with real concern in his voice as he leaves.

I know he's right, and the last thing I want to do is scare off any of our staff or stress them out. If I'm tense or anxious, they're going to pick up on it. So I pack up some of the paperwork to take home with me and text my driver to meet me out front.

I check my phone one more time, but there's still nothing from Gemma.

It's going to be a long fucking night.

Chapter 11
Gemma

I'm pretty sure the car behind me is following me. I just left work, and this car has been behind me ever since. For a moment, I wondered if it was Carter having me followed. But I doubt it because I haven't heard from him since Saturday night. While I don't want to overreact, I decide to call Skye to have someone on the phone with me.

"Hey girl, you coming home after work? I'm about to start dinner."

"Yeah, I'm on my way home now. But I think this car behind me is following me."

"And you called me? Why didn't you call the cops?" Skye asks anxiously.

"Because I'm not sure yet. Just do me a favor and check all the locks, doors, and the windows at the apartment. Make sure everything's locked. I know that I'm going to be a little freaked out for the rest of the night, even if it turns out that they aren't following me."

"Well, don't lead them here. Take a turn and go the long way to see if they follow you."

"Okay, I'm taking the turn to circle back towards the mall."

I work as a jewelry designer at a jewelry store. It's located at the front of the mall surrounded by restaurants, so it seems safe.

When I turn left, so does the car behind me.

"It just turned with me."

"Then turn left again," Skye says.

At the next light, I go left. But this time the car didn't turn with me.

"It kept going," I tell her, and I can hear an audible sigh of relief.

"Get home quickly and safely and don't take your normal route. I'm staying on the phone with you until you get here," she says.

I can hear her moving around, checking the locks on all the windows and the back door.

"Okay, all the locks are good and in place and we'll turn the security system on as soon as you get here."

True to her word, she stays on the phone even as I'm walking in the door. Once the door is closed and locked behind me, she finally hangs up.

"Did you recognize the car? What kind of car was it? Are you sure you weren't followed home?" She rapidly fires some questions at me as I set my purse down.

"No, it was a gray four-door car. Nothing that I recognized and I couldn't see who was driving. After circling around three times, I checked to make sure I wasn't being followed."

"Well, don't be mad," she cringes.

"What did you do?"

"I texted your dad while we were on the phone and told him what was going on. He wants you to call him. Yes, I know I could have just texted Summer, but we both know she would have told your dad, so I just cut out the third person." She hands me a glass of wine like it's going to make everything better.

Taking my phone out, I call him. "Hi, Dad. I'm fine. I think I was just overreacting. For whatever reason, the car gave up and didn't follow me. I circled the block multiple times," I say as soon as my dad picks up the phone.

"Well, it's better to be safe than sorry, sweetheart. Did you turn the alarm on once you were inside?" he asks.

"Yep, Skye made sure of it. She also checked all the doors, locks, and windows and made sure everything was locked up nice and tight."

My dad has money, and when Summer moved in here two years ago, he insisted on installing the alarm system because of how often

I was over. Though he still pays to keep it up, especially now that I'm living here.

"You can always come spend the night and so can Skye, if you don't feel safe. You two are welcome here anytime. You know that."

From the beginning, he wasn't happy about me moving out. Even though he wanted me to stay at the house with him, he was newly married to my best friend. I didn't feel comfortable. Neither did I want them to sneak around or worse, I didn't want to run accidentally into something that I did not want to see. So it was better for everyone this way.

"I know Dad, but I'm fine. If that changes, I promise we'll be knocking at your door regardless of what time it is. I love you. Give Summer a hug for me."

"Love you too, baby," he says.

"Let me change, and then I have something I want to talk to you about," I tell Skye.

After changing into more comfortable clothes, I grab the folder that has the contract in it. Then I join Skye at the dining room table. While I was circling the block multiple times, she had plenty of time to finish up the mac and cheese she was making for dinner.

"Okay, so it's about the guy that I've been seeing at Club Red. Well, he gave me a contract. I've been looking it over, but I'd like to go over it with you since you have much more experience with this stuff."

"Oh, that's so exciting!" Skye's face lights up with a smile. "Before I read this, what are your thoughts on it?"

"Well, I don't know what's normal and what isn't. But I'm guessing it's pretty standard. I talked to Summer about it a little bit at the lunch I had with her and my dad. Fortunately, she said she wasn't going to tell him right now, thank goodness. I don't think I could look him in the eye."

That makes Skye laugh. Opening the folder, she pulls out the contract, glances at page one, and gasps.

"What? What's wrong?"

"The guy you've been seeing is the same guy that gave you this contract?" She asks like she can't believe what she's seeing.

"Yes, why? What's wrong?"

"Carter Morgan is the owner of Club Red. He doesn't play out in the open. I've never seen him with someone, and I've only seen him once from a distance after someone pointed him out. He's so elusive that it's almost become an urban legend that he plays in his club."

I try to reconcile the fact that the Carter that I've been hanging out with is the owner of Club Red. He never let on and I never would have guessed.

"I knew he was rich because he was always in a suit and the way he carried himself in the suit. It wasn't cheap, neither was the watch that he wears. But I just thought that he was some corporate guy with some company. Maybe he was a CEO or something."

"Oh, he's that too. Because that's how he made his money before he opened up the club. His buddy, Hunter, helped him and is a co-owner."

"I have no idea who that is," I admit, refilling my glass.

"Wow, he never told you that he was the club owner?"

"No, we never talk about stuff outside the club."

"So, he doesn't know that your dad is also a member?"

"No. Though he's the owner, I'm sure he can look up my information and maybe put two and two together."

"Whoa, I don't know if I should be ecstatic that my friend bagged the elusive dom, Carter Morgan, or if I'm more than a bit jealous."

She sighs, sits back, and looks over the contract.

Since I'm not sure what to do as she reads through it, I pull out my phone and check my emails and social media.

As anxious as I am to hear her thoughts, Skye takes her time reading over everything, which I appreciate.

"Okay, this is a fairly common contract. Now mind you, every contract is different. But I don't see any red flags here. Because of who he is, of course, he's going to want an NDA. Though I think it's a fairly generous NDA because it allows you to talk to any member, just no one outside of Club Red. So you can still talk to me, your dad, Summer, or anybody at the club."

"That's what Summer said, and I can understand that a lot of people don't know or understand what Club Red is, so they're going to judge a lot harsher."

"Exactly. With his limits, there's nothing crazy or anything you should be aware of. But I want to make sure you see this here. The contract says that you're giving him permission to share you with whoever he wants. That's the only thing that catches my eye."

"Yeah, we've kind of already done that," I say hesitantly, filling her in on what happened on Saturday night.

"Wow, I'm not going to lie. That is hot. Good for you! I love that he's pushing you outside your comfort zone because I know you would have never done anything like that on your own."

She's right. It's way outside my comfort zone, but he seems to know just how far to push me. Because really, there's not a thing that we've done that I didn't like.

"So, either you meet him tomorrow night with this signed contract, or pretty much everything stops. Honestly, I'm surprised he's played with you as much as he has without you having signed the contract."

"Skye, be honest with me. If you were in my shoes, forgetting that Carter owns the club, and he was just any other guy there, would you sign this?"

"I would try to negotiate a few things. But yeah, I would sign. Do you want me to go with you tomorrow and help you advocate a few things?"

"No, I think this is something that I need to do on my own."

"Well, I will keep my phone on me. So, call if you need me, but now let's get on the Club Red forum. Once your part of this contract is filled out, you'll be ready to go.

After spending the rest of the night looking at different limits, checking to see what different things mean, and filling out all the pages on the contract, I think I have ideas. Looking over the health questionnaire that Carter has given to me, I'm thankful that I just had an STD test to get my guest membership at Club Red. It will be good enough for the contract, so I can at least check that off the list.

I have to fill out things like an emergency contact. In which case, I put Skye down and then Summer. There is no way in hell, I'm listing my dad as an emergency contact on my BDSM contract.

Chapter 12
Carter

I'm sitting in a dark little cafe not too far from my office. Even though I love ordering takeout for lunch from this place, I rarely have time to come down and sit in the cafe. Usually my receptionist comes and picks up my order. So, while I eat here often, they won't recognize my face.

After getting here thirty minutes early, I've been anxiously watching the door, willing her to walk in. Never have I been so on edge about someone possibly turning down one of my contracts or having to walk away from them. I'm not sure why I'm this way with Gemma. It could be because we started playing before the contract was signed. Yeah, that has to be it.

Every time the door opens, my eyes shoot up and I'm slightly disappointed when it's not her. A few minutes before the agreed-upon time the door opens, and she walks through. My heart races, and I don't remember the last time I've been so happy and so nervous about something in my entire life.

I'm not used to this feeling. When you're in control of a situation, nerves are not an issue. When she spots me, she smiles and walks over. Standing, I pull out her chair, and running on instinct, I lean in and kiss her on the cheek.

"I'm really glad you came," I tell her. Then, flagging down the server, we order some drinks.

After taking a moment to enjoy each other, she opens up the conversation.

"I haven't signed the contract because there are a few things I want to discuss first."

"Of course, and I'm not assuming that just because you're here that means you're going to sign. But we need to make that decision before we walk out of here tonight."

She nods but doesn't get a chance to answer because the server comes with our drinks.

After we place our order, I begin. "Alright, start whenever you're ready," I give her my full attention.

As she pulls the folder that has the contract out of her bag, she looks around cautiously before speaking.

"First off, I want you to know that I went over this with my roommate. When she saw your name, she knew exactly who you were."

"I had a feeling with her being a regular she would recognize my name. Does that change anything for you?"

"Not really. Honestly, I liked not knowing right away. I was nervous enough as it is."

Her response helps me relax. She's not a gold digger, nor is she one of the women that need the boundaries the contract was created for. However, I do need the boundaries.

"So, I completely understand that this is a Club Red arrangement and I agree with us being exclusive to each other. But Skye said that you also work for a big corporation. If that's the case, will you have some event that you would be taking another woman?" she asks.

It's hard for me to admit, but I kind of like her jealousy over wanting to make sure that no one else is going to be spending time with me because I feel the same way about her.

"No, I'll just go alone. Everyone's used to it by now. In fact, if I showed up with a date, I think that would cause more controversy than going by myself."

"If we're exclusive for any length of time, my dad's going to start asking questions. He's protective because it was just me and him after my mom died. We don't need to have regular dinners or anything, but if after a few months, we decide we want to keep going, I'm going to need you to agree to at least one dinner with my dad just to put his mind at ease."

I don't normally do the whole meet the parents' thing ever for any reason. Normally, that would be a no without even thinking about it. But for some reason, when Gemma asks, I give it pause. Really, it's not an unreasonable request.

But I know her dad from the club, so while it may be awkward, I don't think having dinner with him is going to be a problem.

"I can agree to one dinner."

She makes a note on the contract.

"Make sure you initial any changes you make, and I'll go back in and initial next to them when we're done," I tell her.

"Next, I am very close with my roommate, my dad, and my best friend. We have weekly dinners, and I don't want you interfering with my routine or expecting me to cancel my plans with them. Since this is not an actual relationship and we both know it has an end date, I will choose them over you if you try to force the issue. I also love my job and I won’t have you interfering with it and trying to make me change my schedule for anything."

For a minute, I'm left speechless. Not once has another sub said anything like that to me. Usually they're willing to drop all their plans, thinking that not spending any amount of time with me might make me change my mind. Though my gut twists when she mentions our relationship having an expiration date and it not being permanent.

The thought of her walking away makes me sick. I'm not sure why these contracts don't last forever. But they're meant to have an end date and we get to decide when that end is, but it will end.

Will she stick around the club and let things end with us? Will she find herself another dom? Will I have to watch her with someone else? These are all questions that make my stomach roll. They shouldn't, but they do. But I push all these thoughts aside because right now she's not with anyone else. Right now, she's here with me, and with any luck, the contract will make her mine for the foreseeable future.

"Do you have a passport?" She seems taken aback at my question.

"I do. Why?"

"Because sometimes Club Red does events with other clubs, and as long as we're doing this together, it would be nice to have you come with me. Last month, we did one in Paris. Even though I went alone, I would have enjoyed it more to have someone with me."

"For something like that, I will need plenty of notice. Though I would be happy to go as long as it doesn't interfere with something at work."

After we go over a few more things, including her limits, I produce my STD results from the doctor. I've been given a clean bill of health.

"Before I got my membership, I had to be tested. Even though I haven't been with anyone except for you, I did go back to my doctor and get retested. I know I didn't have to but I wanted a current one for the contract." She pulls out a piece of paper.

Looking it over, I see she has a clean bill of health as well.

We both initial each other's test results to prove that we saw them and slide them into the folder.

When our food comes, we put the contract away and talk, getting to know each other better.

"What made you decide to open up Club Red?" she asks.

"In New York City, I had visited a club like it. But there was nothing here in Chicago, so I saw the need and I had the money to make it happen. Though I didn't have the contacts, but my buddy, Hunter did. So, while the two of us are co-owners, we have several founding members that helped build the place. We all have an equal say in what happens."

"Kind of like a board of directors?"

"Yeah, but we don't use that term. We try to keep it as casual as possible because it's not a paid job." Changing the subject, I ask, "What do you do for work?" Though I already know the answer.

Once I found out who her dad was at the club, I did my research on her. But there's no point in scaring her off and I'll let her tell me what she wants me to know.

"I'm a jewelry designer. My mom loved making jewelry as a hobby, and I remember sitting there for hours handing her beads or watching her do what she did. She taught me everything she knew and answered a million and one of my questions. After she died, I continued doing it because it made me feel closer to her. I knew that there was nothing else I wanted to do for a living and my dad helped me figure out how to make a career out of it and supported me the whole way."

"I'm sorry about your mom," I tell her.

When she gives me a wobbly smile, I quickly change the subject and decide not to push the issue.

"What about you? What do you do outside of owning Club Red?"

Smiling, I don't answer, but keep eating.

"You aren't going to tell me?"

"There are some things that I don't think that we need to talk about. My work life is one of them."

"You know I can just look it up."

"You haven't googled me yet? I'm actually kind of impressed."

"No, but I'm sure my roommate has. And I'm sure she's gone to my best friend and told her, and they've shared some info. So if you have anything that you want to tell me, now is the time. Because the two of them are like dogs with a bone."

"I've got nothing to hide. But I think I'm interested in what they pull up, so I'm going to wait and see."

We go on and talk a bit about her friends and mine. Just casual conversation. Two people on their first date who might want to get to know each other without digging too deep. Yet this is not a first date.

After we're done eating, I circle back to the contract.

"Is there anything else you want to talk about as far as the contract goes, or do you want to tell me if you're going to sign or not?"

"Nope, you answered all my questions. I think I'm ready to sign it if you are."

The way my heart races in my chest when she says that she's going to sign the contract is something I can't remember feeling. Not even the first time I closed my first business deal.

She pulls out the contract and signs it, handing it over to me. Then I initial the changes and each paper before signing on the spot where my name is printed.

"I'll get this taken care of and have a copy for you tomorrow. Tonight Club Red is putting on a private event outside of the club. If you don't have plans, I would be honored if you would join me."

"Wearing this?" She asks, looking down at her T-shirt and jeans that she has on.

While I think she looks gorgeous, it's not the right attire for the event.

"No, wearing this." I hand her the bag that had been sitting next to me on the floor. "Go and change in the bathroom, while I take care of the check."

"Oh here," she tries to hand me her wallet.

I put my hand on her arm. "One thing that wasn't in the contract that maybe I should add is when you're with me, you will never spend a penny. I will cover all costs, dinner, clothes, club fees, and travel."

She hesitates for a moment before she nods, picks up the bag, and heads off to the bathroom to change.

Thankfully, she didn't ask too many questions about the function. Normally, I would have passed on an event outside of Club Red. But with everything going on, I figured her and I could use the extra privacy of not being at the club right now.

Chapter 13

Gemma

Once again, Carter picked out a beautiful dress that fit me perfectly. Thankfully, this one has a lot more coverage than the last one he asked me to wear. Since we're not at Club Red tonight, it makes sense. This dress is a deep navy blue that matches the color of his suit.

The shoes and jewelry that he provided are silver and glittery, and he even had a handbag for me that matched. Impressive, how he had thought of everything. Gathering everything up, I walk back to our table.

While Carter may know how to hide his thoughts, it was written all over his face that he liked what he saw.

Now we’re in the car on the way to this event. I have no idea where we're going, except for the fact that we are heading to a very rich part of town. I'm talking multi-million dollar mansions part of town. I guess this would probably be the area that he lives in, but he made it clear that this wasn't being held at his house. Apparently, it is being put on by a friend of his in conjunction with Club Red.

Carter and I are in the back seat and his driver is battling the traffic for us. While he's checking messages or emails on his phone, Carter has his hand on the inside of my thigh.

"Sorry, I was just checking in on some stuff at Club Red. We have a new guy working there, so I wanted to make sure I stayed on top of it." He puts his phone away just as we turn onto the street where the party is being hosted, which I only know based on the sheer number of cars lining the side of the street.

"Now that we are here, there are a few rules for tonight," he says, waiting for me to make eye contact before he continues.

"You do not leave my side. If you want something to eat or drink or you need to use the restroom, you let me know. We go together. No one else is to touch you without my permission. That's a general rule at any event. Same code words apply. Yellow, red, and green. Also, your Club Red NDA that you signed for your membership applies to this party. Understood?"

"Yes," I say, trying to sound confident. But I must not have pulled it off, as he paused to look at me for a moment.

"We can leave anytime you want. Just say the word. If you walk in there and you don't like the vibe or you feel uncomfortable, we can turn around and walk right back out. Or we can stay for a few hours. It's completely up to you. I will not be upset or disappointed either way."

That calmed my nerves knowing that I don't have to stick it out if I don't want to.

When we arrive, the driver gets out and opens the door for me, giving me his hand to step out. Carter gets out and immediately takes my hand.

We walk up to a large double front door where we're greeted by what looks like security. They must recognize Carter, as we don't even exchange a word just a few head nods. Then they open the door for him.

"Carter! I'm so glad you made it! You don't normally come to these things." A man says as he walks by. He doesn't look my way and Carter doesn't introduce us.

"We aren't going to stay long, as we just came to pop in and show our faces," Carter says. Then we move on and he doesn't even introduce me to the guy.

The entryway of this mansion has a huge statement staircase and there are rooms on either side. We walk to the back where there's a large living area and a bunch of people are gathered. Most of them are naked.

As we enter, Carter puts his arm around my waist and pulls me close to his side. Then he leans down and whispers in my ear. "What color are you at, baby girl?"

"Green. Though I'd love some water."

That seems to please him, and he steers me toward the kitchen and gets me a bottle of water. While he watches me drink, he also keeps an eye on the area.

"There are no private rooms tonight, but I know that this place has a killer pool and back deck. Do you want to head out there?"

"Yeah, I think some fresh air sounds good."

We go out back, and he wasn't kidding about the amazing outdoor space. This is one of those backyard pools that you might see at a resort. There's some beautiful stonework, along with multiple different swimming areas, including a lazy river.

There are multiple seating areas and even a hot tub off to the side. I quickly realize we are the most dressed people here and stick out like a sore thumb.

"Would you like to get in the hot tub?" Carter nods in the direction of the couple getting out, which means we'd have it to ourselves for now, anyway.

"Yes," I say.

He leads us over to a table and we grab towels and set our things right next to the tub. He removes his shoes and socks, along with his jacket. After I have taken off everything but my dress, I hesitate. While he still has quite a few articles of clothing to remove, I'm completely nude under my dress. "Remove the dress and get in the hot tub," he says. His firm, dominant voice sends wetness right to my core.

Turning my back to the crowd, I move so that only he can see the front of me. Then, doing as he says, I take a deep breath and get into the hot tub. When I glance around, not one person is watching me. I feel completely exposed, even though everyone else is completely naked. But I guess one more person without clothes won't draw any attention.

Once I get settled in the hot tub, I get to enjoy the view of Carter undressing piece by piece. He's watching me, watching him. Then, smirking he starts rolling up the sleeves of his button-down shirt and moves to stand behind me.

"You aren't getting in?" I ask.

Instead, he puts his hands on my shoulders and begins rubbing them.

"There's not going to be enough room for me," he says just as two guys walk up.

I wonder if this has anything to do with the hard limit in the contract about him not taking his shirt off, and me not trying to remove it. Curiously, in the contract, it was one of his limits. Though I know this isn't the place to ask.

"Would you gentlemen care to join us?" Carter asks.

No names are given. But they reply instantly, "Yes, we would," as they climb into the hot tub in front of me.

These guys are pretty big, and Carter's right, if he had been in here, space would be very limited.

"Touching only," he says to the men.

Then he leans down to whisper in my ear. "My rule still applies. Don't break it."

I nod my head as my nerves start to get the better of me.

One guy looks really out of place, like he's a surfer visiting from California. He has a hairless chest, a tan for days, with a very distinct tan line at his waist, and not a single tattoo.

In contrast, the other guy has dark brown hair, a beard, a tattoo, and more of a farmer's tan. He's got hair on his chest, and just like his friend, he has an amazing set of chiseled abs.

The guys move with each sitting on either side of me. Neither of them says a word to me, just like the last time. I assume this is out of respect for Carter.

They each take one of my breasts in their hands and start playing with it. With Carter's hands still on my shoulders, I lean my head back onto his stomach, closing my eyes and enjoying the sensations.

The blonde guy on my right rests his hand on my thigh under the water before slowly moving upward to rub between my thighs. His friend hooks my other leg over his knees, spreading me out.

When the blond guys plays with my clit, the pleasure ramps up.

I moan and move my hips to the rhythm of his fingers as I feel my orgasm begin to build. The other guy is still playing and squeezing my breasts as Carter continues to massage my shoulders.

The sensations become too much for me and I try to refocus my thoughts. The blond guy lets up and removes his hand, but I only have a moment's rest before the guy on my left has his hand between my legs.

Carter grips my hair and pulls my head back, as the other guy fingers me. Once again I can feel the tension in my body build and my pussy fluttering, as the guy on my left continues fingering me faster and faster. When I'm about to come apart, he slowly slides two fingers into me, while Carter kisses my neck.

The sensations are all too much for me and I let out a moan as I feel pleasure radiating through my body. I'm so close, but the guy on my left stops and takes his hand away, leaving me feeling unfulfilled.

"Thank you, gentleman," Carter says, dismissing them.

"No, thank *you*, Carter." The surfer guy says as they get out of the water, grab towels, and walk off as I try to catch my breath.

Just then, another man walks up and speaks to Carter.

"I couldn't believe it when I heard that Carter Morgan was here. Knew you'd have a freebie," he says.

He's eyeing me up, but his gaze is icky and dirty. For the first time tonight, I feel the need to cover myself.

"I'm not sharing her with you, Lucas," Carter says, his voice cold.

Before I know it, he's handing me a towel.

"Come on. Get out of the hot tub," he says, while wrapping the towel around me and shielding me from Lucas' eyes.

"Go ahead and get dressed. I'll hold the towel for you," he says softly.

While he holds the towel, I have some privacy, so I grab another towel to dry off and quickly slip my dress back on.

Once my dress is on, Carter sets the towel down. Kneeling, he takes my shoes and helps me put them on. Quickly, I put my jewelry into my purse. Then Carter slips on his shoes without the socks, carrying his jacket and socks in one hand, while firmly wrapping his arm around my waist.

"So, this is how it's going to be?" Lucas says as we walk away.

"This is how you made it. I'm not sure how you even got into this event, but rest assured, I will make sure that you won't be at any future ones."

With that, Carter guides me back into the house.

Carter is extremely tense beside me, but I don't say anything as we go straight to the door, ignoring everyone else. His driver is already waiting for us outside with the door open. I wonder to myself how he knew to be there just when we needed him.

I slide into the car and Carter gets in behind me and doesn't relax until the car door is closed. I'm unsure what to do. We don't talk much about our private lives, but there are a million questions floating around in my head.

Taking Carter's hand in mine, I want to offer a bit of silent strength. He gives my hand a gentle squeeze and looks over at me.

"He's an ex-employee of Club Red. And there's a very good reason why. Not only was he not very good at following the rules, but he made multiple women uncomfortable. Like he did to you tonight," he says without me even having to ask.

"How did you know I was uncomfortable?" I had not said a single word to him.

"I'm always watching your body language. As soon as he spoke, you tried to cover yourself up. Even if you hadn't, I would have gotten you out of there immediately. I don't want you in his presence, and you aren't safe around him. Your safety is my number one priority for as long as you're with me."

Now I'm not sure what to say. I know Carter is always aware of what's going on around us. Though my mind is always focused on other things.

Shifting in his seat, he faces me, taking both of my hands in his, and looks me right in the eye.

"I know you're new to all this, but it is always your Dom's responsibility to ensure your safety above all else, not just from me, but also making sure that you're comfortable with what's going on and respecting your safe words. When you see other people like we do, it's important to keep you from unsafe people. Even though I've already said this, your safety will come before all else. Before your pleasure, before my pleasure, whether you like it or not."

Biting my lip, I think about what he just said as the car pulls out onto the main road.

"I do feel safe with you, which is big for me because I don't feel safe with a lot of people." Somehow, he knows I don't want to talk about it and I'm glad he doesn't ask questions. Already I've revealed more than I reveal to most people.

"Now, I never have any intention of leaving you unsatisfied," he says with a slightly wicked glint in his eye.

Then he presses a button and the privacy screen between us and the driver goes up.

Moving to the floor, he kneels in front of me, pushing my dress up before slinging both of my legs over his shoulders.

He starts with slow, gentle, teasing licks, and I can feel my body relax as he explores my body with his tongue. His lips lightly brush over my clit as he flicks his tongue over it. All the tension from earlier leaves my body as a wave of pleasure radiates through me. The orgasm he denied me earlier starts creeping back.

Moving faster with intensity, he flicks my clit until I'm on the brink of an orgasm. Then he slows back down.

He knows exactly how to keep me right on that edge as he continues to tease, lick, and nibble at my most intimate areas.

When his fingers slowly slide into me, I can't help but cry out in pleasure. His eyes sparkle with delight as he watches my body tremble with each touch. I can feel the intensity of his gaze as it sweeps across my body, making it impossible for me to keep still.

Desperate for release, I'm panting now and holding on by a hair. Carter knows it, and slides his fingers out of me, gently kissing the inside of my thighs.

"Carter!" I whine, feeling him smile against the inside of my thigh.

He looks up at me before sucking on my clit again. This time I run my hands through his hair trying to prevent him from stopping again.

Taking my cue, he moves his fingers back inside me, curling them up towards my G-spot. His tongue circles around it as I moan louder.

Slow waves of spasms build until I'm unable to contain it anymore and I fall over the edge into an intense orgasm. Carter continues to caress and lick my body until every pulsing explosion between my thighs has dwindled.

After slowly moving from between my legs, he pulls my dress down. There's a satisfied smirk on his face, and I guess he's earned it. Then he leans in for a passionate kiss that leaves both of us breathless once again.

I can taste myself on his lips, and it sends a shiver down my spine. He pulls away and looks into my eyes with an intensity that leaves me speechless.

Not knowing what to say, I reach for him to try and return the favor.

He stops me before I can even reach his belt.

Smiling, he shakes his head. "Not tonight, baby girl," he says softly, caressing my cheek with the back of his hand. "Tonight was all about you."

For the rest of the ride, I enjoy being snuggled in his arms. When the car stops, I look up and see we are outside my apartment.

"I had one of my guys bring your car back here. He left the keys with your roommate," he says before I can say anything.

He's very much a take-charge person and I'm just not used to that, but I also know there's no point in arguing with him.

"You said something about needing to learn how to be a sub. Well, there's a woman at the club, her name is Pink, and she works with new subs. I set up a meeting for you with her Thursday night at Club Red at seven o'clock." He hands me a card with the information written down on it.

Before I think to speak, he stops me.

"I know you said not to make plans and expect you to change them, but this is the only time slot she had available for the next few weeks." He's looking a bit shy, which is unusual for him.

"I was going to say thank you and that I will be there," I say.

Smiling, he helps me out of the car and walks me up to the door. After kissing me on the cheek, he watches me walk inside.

Normally, I would hate someone making an appointment for me. That it doesn't bother me, tells me this man is going to be dangerous.

Chapter 14
Carter

Today I can't seem to concentrate on a damn thing. All that runs through my mind is the party last night. I've already talked to the guy who threw it, and it turns out Lucas came as a guest with one of the members. He had not been invited himself. The member who invited him has been notified that Lucas is not welcome at any club events. If it happens again, their membership will be suspended indefinitely. We don't play around with people's safety. But when it comes to Gemma's safety, there's nothing I won't do. It's a new feeling for me, and it's stronger than just the usual dom keeping his sub safe. It's much stronger.

That's why I have an almost feral need to have eyes on her. I've placed a full-time security detail on her. I want someone watching her house and the jewelry store to make sure she's okay.

I check in with her security guy again. When Hunter comes in, he closes the door and sits down.

"What in the hell happened at the party last night?" He says not even wasting time with hellos.

"I guess that depends upon who you talk to."

"Who haven't I talked to? At this point, the entire staff has heard about it and they all have different theories about what is going on. But since none of them are willing to come and talk to you directly, here I am. I want to hear it straight from the source," he says, crossing his arms and staring me down, letting me know that he's serious about this one.

"Gemma signed the contract," I start.

A big grin crosses his face. "Good. I know you like her, but if you need the contract to feel comfortable having any type of relationship with her, then I'm all for it."

Normally I would hound him on that, but today I just let it slide. It's not a relationship and I'm pretty sure at this point he does it just to mess with me.

"Well, afterward we went to the party we sponsored, and everything was going well. We had some time in the hot tub."

"You got in the hot tub?" Hunter sounds shocked, and I can understand why he would be. Getting in water means removing clothes, and that's something I don't do, and he knows why.

"No, Gemma got in the hot tub, and I was there with her."

"Standing behind her fully clothed like a creeper?" Hunter asks.

"Fully clothed, but not like a creeper, thank you. But after we'd had some fun, of all people, Lucas showed up. He tried to push his way into the scene and interact with Gemma. But I quickly shut it down, got her dressed, and we left."

"Shit, what was he even doing there? Let me make some phone calls and we'll get this taken care of." He pulls out his phone, but I stop him.

"First thing this morning, I made those calls. He was there as a guest of another member. I made it very clear to that member that Lucas was let go from Club Red for safety reasons and was not to be at any one of these events again. If that rule was broken, her membership would be permanently revoked. She wasn't happy, and I guarantee you that'll be the end of whatever sugar mama cougar relationship that they have."

"We need to tighten security at these events, too. He shouldn't have been able to get in the door."

"I agree, but we don't have the same technology at these parties as we do here at the club to run cards and names."

Hunter knows I'm right because our client list doesn't leave this property. So even having access to it on another device at a party like that is not an option. It's another safeguard for our members.

"I hate to think we have to call everyone in here to verify that they and their guests are welcome. That seems like a lot of work and many people may not jump through the hoops to go to these off-site parties."

"Even though I agree, at this point, we've got to come up with something. Last night could have been a very bad situation," I tell him.

He nods his head because he knows it's true.

I continue, "We've been very lucky here at Club Red. Mostly we've had to deal with firing a few employees, and throwing out some people who took things a little too far or made other members uncomfortable. Though, we've also kicked out a few people for abusing the drink maximum and getting trashed. And we suspended one membership due to a lack of payment."

We haven't had any real problems that have infringed on the safety of our members and their guests. There haven't been any assaults or anything that someone felt the need to press charges. Though we've made it very clear to everyone they are welcome to press charges and we have a protocol in place if that were to happen. But Hunter and I both know we've been very lucky that we haven't had to use it. The first time that we do, sure as hell, is not going to be because Gemma is the one that presses charges.

Over my dead body.

"Since you seem to have that under control, the new marketing intern is here. I thought maybe we'd go down and introduce ourselves," Hunter says, knowing that I want to meet the guy too.

Getting up, I follow him out of the office and down the hall to the marketing department. Cade is pretty much in charge of this department, and he does well with it. He may be young, but that just means he's more up-to-date on all the social media and the new marketing techniques online. So both Hunter and I are more than happy to turn that department over to him.

Though if anything were to happen, it's our necks on the line, so we stay up to date on all aspects of it. As we get ready to round the corner, we can hear Seth talking to someone and I put my hand on Hunters' shoulder, silently stopping him. Neither of us says a word.

"If you pay attention, kid, it'll be easy to work your way up. There is much to learn. Mainly I took this job so that I can do something I like, but I also can learn how to manage my own club. Because someday I plan on opening mine," Seth says.

I assume he's talking to the intern, Kyle.

Hunter looks back over at me, and I point to my eyes indicating he needs to keep right on him. He nods that he gets it.

Later, I plan to remind Seth of his non-compete clause. He's free to open up his club when he leaves here if he has the money, but it won't be in Chicago.

His non-compete strictly states that he cannot work for another club within a two-hundred mile radius of Club Red. Nor can he open his club within a five-hundred mile radius of any Club Red location. That means he'd have to be as far away as Atlanta or even Washington, DC.

When the time is right, I have plans to expand Club Red. Right now, I have my eye on Las Vegas, along with a few other cities around the country.

Anyway, I don't know where Seth would get the money to open his club. He doesn't have any money, and neither does his family. One thing I do know, is we sure as hell are not paying him enough to save up for that kind of investment unless he's got someone with deep pockets willing to back him, which I don't see happening because Seth is not the kind of person to make those types of connections.

But still, something just doesn't sit right in my gut about him. So I'm not going to turn my back or just dismiss it. I learned the hard way to listen and I've got the scars to prove it.

Removing my hand from Hunter's shoulder, we walk into the room like we hadn't just heard what was going on. I take slight satisfaction in the fact that Seth instantly looks a bit uncomfortable, like he's not sure if we heard anything. Though we continue to act like we hadn't, and he soon relaxes.

"Hey, we wanted to come in and meet Kyle. Put a face to the name that Cade has told us so much about," Hunter says, holding out his hand to shake Kyle's hand.

I do the same, and my first instinct on the kid is that he's young, but he seems to be able to hold his own, which is an A plus in this business.

"Appreciate the chance to work here. I think it's going to be the perfect test of my abilities," he says awkwardly.

Cade said that this guy is really smart, so I guess the awkwardness comes with the territory, which is completely fine with me. People skills can be learned from paying attention, but the smarts to do his job, not so much.

"Hopefully, Seth here gave you a tour of the place so that you know what we do. That tour should have included my office. If you ever need anything, have a question or even some ideas to improve the club, feel free to stop in. If I'm not there, leave a note with my secretary and I will make sure to come find you," I tell him.

"I gave him the tour and the rundown of how everything works. But I also told him you guys were not to be bugged unless it was a big deal. Otherwise, he can come to me with any issues or questions." Seth tries to redirect him, and I catch it. It's as if he doesn't want Kyle coming to me or Hunter about anything.

When I look over at Hunter, I can tell just by his expression that he picked up on it, too.

"Honestly, we don't mind. We have an open-door policy here and anyone is welcome to come in and talk to us. Don't worry, we're not going to bark at you about the chain of command or anything like that," Hunter says, keeping eye contact with Kyle.

"I appreciate it," Kyle says with a forced smile.

We're starting to make him uncomfortable, which is our cue to get the hell out of here.

"Well, we'll see you around, Kyle. Hope you enjoy working here. We like to think that it's a great place to work, so hopefully you'll want to stick around," I say.

Once we're back in the hallway heading towards our offices, I look over at Hunter.

"That was weird, right? It wasn't just me?" I ask.

"No, that was odd. I'll do some poking around," he sighs.

Though I know he would rather look into it, and it be nothing, than ignore it and it'd be a bigger issue.

"By the way, I set Gemma up with a meeting with Pink," I told him.

"I think that's a great idea. You said she's new to all this, so it's always good to have some help and guidance from someone outside the dynamic."

"That was my thought, too. I know she has her friend, Skye. But in case there's anything she's afraid to talk to her about, I'd rather her have another ally here at the club. Plus, I know Pink will start at the beginning and make sure to cover everything."

"I have not seen you go through this much trouble for anyone else you've had a contract with," he says, pausing outside my office.

"I've never had a new sub before. Usually, they all have experience."

"I don't think that's it. At any time, you could have turned around and walked away if you didn't want a new sub. But you've never wanted someone new to all this before. She's special and you see it. Just don't overlook how unique she is and let her slip away," he says before continuing down the hall.

I have no idea what in the bloody hell he means. While I know Gemma is special, I plan to hold on to her for as long as she allows. But what we have has an expiration date. At some point, we will walk away from each other.

Chapter 15

Gemma

Today is my meeting with Pink. I'm excited and nervous, but Carter trusts her, so I need to trust him. Skye said she's heard good things about her, but she's never worked with her. That prompted me to ask Skye how she got into all this, and she just shrugged her shoulders and gave me a smirk before changing the subject. After that, I decided not to push it.

It's about three o'clock in the afternoon, and I'm meeting Pink at Club Red. It's a bright sunny day, but in the parking lot I have a sense of unease. Like there's someone watching me. I don't get out of my car right away. I look around to check things out. Seeing the security cameras, I think maybe that's what I'm feeling. Could be someone's watching on the security cameras. Though I don't see another single soul, so I take a deep breath, shake it off and go inside.

"Hey, sweetheart; Pink is ready for you by the stage. Same rules as if you were here during club hours." The receptionist tells me with a smile.

After putting my stuff away in the locker room, I go into the main area. The club has a very different feel during the day. The lights are up and it's nice and bright and you can see more of the room's detail. There are wet floor signs and the smell of whatever they used to clean.

I guess when you own a sex club, and sex is being had on every surface, deep cleaning is essential pretty much every day. Even though the thought had never crossed my mind, I'm glad they stay on top of it.

When I make my way toward the stage, I see a tiny little woman that almost looks like a pixie sitting at one of the tables. She has short hair, and it's dyed a bright pink. I guess that's how she got her name.

"You must be Gemma. Carter has told me all about you." Smiling, she gets up and offers me her hand to shake.

"That's me, and that must make you Pink," I say, shaking her hand.

"Yep, that's me. Let's have a seat and get to know each other."

When I take a seat at the table, there's already a bottle of water there for me.

"So, I'd like to start the session off by getting to know your story. What got you here, and I'll share some of mine. Only share what you're comfortable with, though I'd love to know what brought you right now to Club Red."

She's so friendly that I can't help but want to tell her.

Plus, I don't want to let Carter down. I know he wants me to benefit from this meeting as well.

"My roommate is a member here and she and I have been friends for a while. We read a book series on a sex club that I loved, and we got to talking about it more and more. But I was in a relationship with a guy who was as vanilla as they come. The relationship progressed, and he asked me to marry him. Though not too long after I accepted his proposal, things just didn't feel right, so I called off my engagement. At the same time, my best friend announced her engagement to my dad."

"Holy shit, I did not see that one coming. How did you feel about that?" She says with a hint of laughter in her voice.

"When I first found out, I was more upset at how I discovered it, by stumbling upon them versus them telling me. But it's plain to see how happy they make each other, and I want that for both of them. My dad was young when he found out his girlfriend was pregnant. He did the right thing by marrying my mom. But she died when I was young, and I have not seen him with anyone since.

I'm not going to lie. It was awkward when she moved in. Since her roommate was Skye, I moved in with her, and Summer moved in with my dad."

"Your dad is Knox? And Summer is now your new stepmom? I know them well. They're members here, so that has got to be uncomfortable."

"Now they mostly only come for special events and things like that. Since Summer knows that I have been coming here on a regular basis, she has told me that when they make plans to come, she will let me know. Plus, I'm pretty sure that Skye set up something in the system to let us know if the other is here when we try to check in."

"If Skye didn't, then I'm sure Carter did."

I shrug it off because I doubt he did. But I don't want to get into that debate right now.

"Well, after the broken engagement, Skye dragged me here to Club Red. She said I needed to at least explore it now that I was free. On my first night here, I met Carter. Though I had no idea who he was. We just had fun together, and that night led to another and here we are. I'm pretty sure he set this up because he knows I know nothing. I've been kind of flying by the seat of my pants, and from what Skye has told me."

"Well, each dynamic is different, and Carter gave me an outline of yours and what he'd like us to go over. Right now, I'd like to tell you a little bit about me so you can understand where I'm coming from too."

"Of course." I like that she's willing to share about herself and not make this completely one-sided. It's harder to open up when you feel like you're the only one sharing.

"I, too, was in a very vanilla relationship, and it took me a long time to realize it was never going to be enough for me. I joined the social media website that Club Red now owns. But back then, it was not owned by Club Red, and it was just talking and 'let's see what was out there.' By talking to other people, it made me not feel quite so alone. Then I saw some people mentioning Club Red. When a sub friend I had made invited me to come with her under the protection of her and her Dom to check it out. So I did. Instantly, I knew I couldn't go back to a vanilla relationship. After I ended things, she hooked me up with a dom who was willing to train me. However, that sub is no longer here because she and her dom were transferred for his job.

Through trying different things, I learned a lot about what I liked and didn't like. My relationship with that dom was only sexual. While I was under his protection, I met my current partner and my dom. He was the one that realized that I would be good at training and helping new subs in the club. He was right. I love being able to help people. There's a lot to learn, and the more you know, the fewer people can take advantage of you. The BDSM lifestyle can have a bad rap, and I don't want that to ever stop someone from getting to know who they truly are."

Even though I can tell there are points in her story that she's glossed over, it's not my place to push to hear about it.

"Today, I don't want to assume that you know anything. So we're just going to go over all the basics of what a dynamic looks like. Also, the rules here at Club Red and any red flags that you need to watch out for. Not that I think you'll see any with Carter because he is one of the truly good guys. Though if at any point you move on with another dom, I want you to know what you should be watching out for."

The next hour we spend going over everything. Before I left, she gave me a book to take home and read that she says was life-changing for her. It explains parts of different dynamics and different kinks.

It's still daylight as I'm getting ready to leave, and once again, as I step out of Club Red, I have that familiar feeling that I'm being watched. Looking around, I see nothing. So once again, I shake it off and make my way out to my car with my keys in my hand. I'm two rows away when someone grabs my arm from behind.

Spinning around, my heart racing, I come face to face with my ex-fiancé, Dustin. When I see his familiar face, I relaxed.

"Dustin. You scared the crap out of me. What are you doing here?"

"I can't believe you are into this stuff," he says.

Something about his tone puts me on high alert. Something isn't right.

"What are you talking about?"

"Is this why you dropped me? Because you want to be raped every night? Well, all you had to do was speak up. At least I could do that for you," he growls.

What Pink said earlier about how not everyone understands what happens at Club Red flashes into my mind.

At this point, Dustin has me backed up against some car, out of sight of the road.

"That's not what the club is about." I try to educate him, but when he reaches between us and tries to undo my pants, fear truly sets in.

Fighting back, I push his shoulders, but he is too strong for me to even get him to budge. So, I kick and yell stop over and over again.

"That's how you like it, huh? Putting up a little fight? I can handle this." He forcibly pins me to the car.

This time, when I try to shove him away, he goes flying across several empty parking spots. Standing there in shock, I wonder how the hell I managed it. Until someone moves to stand between me and Dustin, so he can't get back to me.

After a moment, I realized it was Carter. After running my hands over my hair and fixing my clothes, I peer around him. Two security guys have Dustin pinned to the ground.

"Come on; she wanted this. I'm her fiancé," Dustin yells.

Carter's body stiffens at Dustin's words.

"Ex-fiancé. We broke up before my dad and Summer even got married. And no, I didn't want this. Hence, the telling you to stop and pushing you away."

Carter steps between us again, this time facing me.

"Let these guys deal with him. Come back inside to my office," he says softly.

I shake my head. "I'd rather go home."

"Then let me take you home and arrange to get your car to you later."

Hesitating for a moment, I decide that not driving right now sounds like a smart thing to do. My head is spinning, so I give him my car keys, which are still in my hand after all this.

Wrapping an arm around my waist, he directs me to his car.

He doesn't have a driver today, but he helps me into the front seat and buckles me up before turning and getting into the car himself.

We drive for a few minutes in silence before the need to fill the silence gets overwhelming.

"I don't know what got into him. He was not like that when we were together."

"There's a lot of misunderstandings around this world and all things to do with BDSM and what it involves," Carter says.

"That's what Pink said. I just didn't think...."

I pause, not sure what words to use next. Maybe the events of the day are starting to catch up with me.

"You didn't think that you'd have to explain it so soon to someone?" Carter tries to finish the sentence for me, and I nod.

"I wish I could say it won't happen again, but it will over and over. I just hope that I'm around to deal with it for you. But I will make sure there are no more nights like tonight.

"You know, I should have had someone walk me out. I had this feeling someone was watching me on the way into the club, and I had the same feeling when I stepped out earlier. But I didn't see anyone, so I blew it off. Oh God, I wonder if he was the one that tried to follow me home the other day." My mind starts racing.

Carter hits the brakes and pulls the car off onto the side of the road.

"Someone tried to follow you home the other day?" He turns to look at me.

"When I left work, there was this car following me. It was not a big deal. I called Skye, made a few turns, and took a long way home. The car disappeared. When I got home, I called my dad and told him about it. Until tonight, things had been nice and quiet. Shit, I'm going to have to call my dad and tell him about this. He is not going to be happy," I say, my mind racing.

"Gemma. Look at me." His tone is firm and leaves no room for argument.

"When you think someone's following you or you get any inclination that something isn't right, like someone's watching you, call me. It is my job to protect you in and out of the club."

"In the end, they didn't follow me. What would you have done if it was the middle of the week? You were at work, it never occurred to me to bother you."

"You are never a bother, and I would have sent someone to escort you home safely. The same way, if you had said something tonight, I would have taken you to your car myself."

"I didn't even know you were at the club."

"Security knew."

Since I don't want to argue anymore or talk about this, I'm hoping that if I agree, he'll just drop it.

"Next time I think someone's following me or that someone might be watching me, I promise you will be the first one to know."

"Thank you." He gets the car back on the road, but then reaches over and takes my hand. The rest of the way home, he's running his thumb over the back of my hand and it's so relaxing that I could almost fall asleep.

Parking the car, he helps me out and walks me up to my front door.

"Be ready at five tomorrow. I'll be picking you up. Yes, I know I'm not asking, but after today, just let me." His voice is gentle, not demanding.

Agreeing, I say, "Make it 5:30 so that I have time to get ready after work and you have a deal."

"I'll be here at five and you take as long as you want to get ready," he says, smiling.

"Fine, see you tomorrow."

He leans in and I expect a kiss on the cheek, but this time it's a soft kiss on the lips. Unfortunately, it's over before I can even register what's happening.

Something's changed in him. Something shifted. I can feel it, though I have no idea what it is. But we are going to the club early tomorrow and I'm kind of excited to see why.

Chapter 16
Carter

As I pull up to Gemma's house, I once again question what the hell I'm doing. Though I don't try to talk myself out of it, I just get out of the car and walk up to her door and knock. Her roommate answers the door.

"You must be Carter," she says.

Then she makes no move to hide the fact that she's looking me over. Probably clocking every detail in case she needs to give my description to the authorities. Somewhere along the way, I've heard she's a firecracker.

"And you must be the roommate, Skye," I say, making her frown.

"Roommate and friend," she says, stepping aside to let me in.

The apartment's nice, and it's decorated showing the two women that live here. There are pink throw pillows on the couch, and a pink rug on the living room floor. Pictures are scattered everywhere. Many in glittery picture frames.

Though her apartment is small compared to where I live, it has more warmth and liveliness in it. It feels more like a home than any place I can remember living.

"Have a seat. She'll be out in a few minutes," she says, sitting on one end of the couch.

So I sit down on the other end.

Neither of us says anything, but a few minutes later Gemma appears. But she's dressed like she's ready to go to Club Red.

"Where do you think we're going today, baby girl?" I ask.

She shrugs. "The club, where else?"

"We're not going to the club. Go put on a different dress. Something that you would wear to dinner."

After looking at me for a moment, she shakes her head and disappears back down the hallway to where I'm sure her room is.

"Where are you taking her?"

"I figured after last night she could use a bit of spoiling. I'm also pretty sure you have a tracking app on her phone, so you'll be able to follow us the whole time."

She smiles at that and nods.

Gemma comes back out in a stunning green cocktail dress, looking at me hesitantly.

"You look perfect and absolutely beautiful. Are you ready to go?"

She nods at me, smiling.

Taking her hand, I lead her out to the parking lot where my driver is waiting for us, and help her into the car.

"Is this another one of those parties like the mansion party?" she asks

It's no wonder she's thinking like that. But I know she'll like what I have planned.

"Just wait. I think you'll enjoy it."

At my words, she nods, relaxing back into her seat.

While I know she'll enjoy what I have planned, but not for the first time today, I start second-guessing it. I'm not sure why I'm doing a date night other than I feel like she deserves it. Especially after what she went through yesterday. She deserves to know that not all men are like her ex, and I want her to know how she should be treated.

At least I keep telling myself that it's because I want her to find a good guy when we move on from our contract. Yet I still don't like the thought of it.

We pull up in front of the aquarium, which was closed for the day.

"Oh, I haven't been here since I was a kid. We were learning about marine biology in school and my dad brought me and we did a bunch of behind-the-scenes tours. But isn't it closed today?" she asks, looking around.

Opening her door, I take her hand and lead her to one of the side doors. A security member is there and lets us in.

"Right this way, Mr. Morgan," the security guy says, leading us down a hallway and through several exhibits. Finally, we end up at an underwater tunnel where the fish are swimming overhead. Usually, it's for visitors to walk through.

Tonight, it's transformed with a table and chairs with an elegant dinner prepared. The sharks and fishes are still swimming around above us. Though it looks like tonight, they're putting on a show for just us.

As we walk into the tunnel, she's looking up at the fish swimming over us. When we reach the table, I pull out a chair for her. She stops short, looks at me, and then she looks around like she's truly seeing the setup for the first time. For some reason, I'm nervous.

"Did you do all this for me?" She looks at the table and then back at me.

"I figured after yesterday you deserved something nice and to know that not all guys are huge creeps like your ex."

Smiling, she kisses me gently on the cheek before sitting down and allowing me to push her chair in.

I take the seat across from her and she smiles at me. Then, looks back up at the fish. I'm pleased that she seems mesmerized by it, which gives me a sense of pride that I picked something that she likes.

Over dinner, we talk about simple things. She tells me about a client she's working with to design an engagement ring. How she's working with another man who's come to design a necklace for his wife for their fiftieth wedding anniversary. The way her face lights up when she talks about her job, I can see how much she loves it.

By the time we're eating dessert, the conversation circles back to her ex.

"Dustin wasn't always like the guy that you met yesterday. He used to be nice and caring, holding the car door open for me. When I was in the middle of finals, he would bring me food to make sure I ate." She pauses, taking a bite of the dessert, and looks lost in thought for a moment.

"His parents lived about an hour and a half from school, so we used to go and visit them a lot. I loved visiting them. His mom would cook these delicious homemade meals and we'd have card games or movie nights. It was a nice change of pace. Later, Skye made me realize that I enjoyed hanging out with his family more than I enjoyed hanging out with him. It made me think.

When he proposed during a family BBQ, I said yes. I was so excited to go home and tell Dad. We went home early, and I came up with breakfast and that's when I found out about Summer."

"Summer is the best friend that he's now married to?"

"Yep. I didn't handle it well. When she walked in with nothing on but my dad's T-shirt, I was shocked and angry. Eventually, my dad and I talked. I realized when he said he planned to marry Summer, that I was more excited about Dad marrying her, than I was to marry Dustin. Then I came to find out Dustin didn't even talk to my dad beforehand. So Dad had no clue that he was going to propose, which didn't sit right with me because Dustin knew how close my dad and I were and always had been. It still took me a few weeks before I was able to call everything off. Yesterday was the first time I've seen him since we broke up."

I don't want her ex to put a damper on the mood, so I change the subject as we finish up dessert.

After the aquarium, we move downtown and take a walk along the river. It was pleasant walking around, enjoying people-watching and everything going on downtown. Since she opened up, I figured it was my turn.

"Right out of high school, I joined the military and loved what I did. After my first deployment, I started dating a girl and thought she could have been the one. Then I got orders to deploy, and it was nice to have letters and care packages and someone who I could call. I knew as soon as I got home from that deployment, I was going to propose.

A month before we were to come home, we were out on patrol and were ambushed. Unfortunately, the information we had been given was wrong. It was just bad all the way around. We had to fight our way out of there."

We stop and wait for someone in front of us to take a picture and then move around them.

"I refused to leave anyone behind, and we all made it out alive. But I have a lot of scars on my chest and my back from where I was cut and sliced trying to get my men out. Needless to say, I had never been so happy to go Stateside again.

She was there waiting for me and went to my doctor's visits. My scars aren't pretty and the first time she saw them, the cuts were still pretty fresh and healing. After getting a good look at them, she said it was too much and broke up with me.

That's the one thing I wanted you to know about are the scars. Few people have seen my scars. Some are disgusted by them. Some I could see the pity on their faces. After that, I never wanted to be vulnerable again. Hence the contracts."

I smile at her, trying to ease the tension. But at the same time, I'm also waiting for her to pull away. Instead, she squeezes my hand and pulls me closer. The emotion that clogs my throat is almost too much.

"Is that what made you want to start Club Red?"

"Partly. My mom was a single mom, and we grew up poor. I mean so poor that many times Mom wouldn't eat just so that I could. By joining the military, I was able to stay in the barracks and had no expenses other than my phone or if I wanted to leave the post. That way I was able to send money back to Mom to help her out, and to get her a better apartment.

While I was in the military, I finished up my schooling. I had this idea for an app, and Hunter, who is my partner at the club and was also one of my best friends from boot camp, was great at coding. So we put my idea together, and a year after being discharged from the military, we sold it for several million dollars. That money we used to build the next app. Hunter is the one that's great at managing Club Red. But it was my idea and planning that started it. Club Red was meant to be a safe place."

"Well, you've made it a safe place," she says as we stop to look out over the water. "Are the scars the reason you have the part in the contract about not taking off your shirt? Is that why you wouldn't get in the hot tub with me the other night?"

All I can do is nod.

When she nods in acceptance, her eyes lock with mine. She lifts her hand and before she even moves it, I know what she's going to do. My mind races and panics. Though, I figure if I'm going to scare her off, now would be the time to do it.

Then, slowly, she moves her hands toward my chest and gently slips it under my coat jacket. With a delicate touch, she rests her hand on the center of my chest.

Over the years, just a simple touch on my chest would make my skin crawl, but not with her. So carefully I move her hand over to one of the scars that I know she'll be able to feel through my shirt.

Slowly she traces it, and I don't move a muscle. I don't dare break the trance. I enjoy this moment in time when someone is not repulsed by the scars.

When she's done tracing the scar, her eyes look back up at me. "You'll find I don't scare easily, I have scars too. Mine are more on the inside and easily hidden."

I lean in and kiss her. Truly kiss her in a tender way that I haven't until now.

She grips my shirt and pulls me closer to her. I'm shocked she isn't pushing me away.

Cupping the back of her head, I'm desperate to taste more of her. To feel her body against mine. Someone walking by clears their throat, and I suddenly remember that we are still in public.

Reluctantly, I pull away, but I don't like that it's over.

"Meet me at Club Red tomorrow night?" I ask, desperate to see her again.

When she agrees, I take her home.

I have some planning to do.

Chapter 17

Gemma

When I get home from work, there's a box sitting on my doorstep. It looks just like the box Carter sent me last time with something to wear to Club Red. Smiling, I check the box and sure enough, it's addressed to me. I take it inside and open it to find a stunning red dress that has glitter embedded in the fabric. The dress may be too generous of a word for this garment. I'm pretty sure that this is just a fancy piece of lingerie. Because when I hold it up, there's no way it would even cover my butt.

It is skintight, just like the last one, with a plunging neckline. There's a note from him, so I open it. But before reading it, I take a minute to run my finger over his beautiful handwriting.

Gemma,

Wear only this tonight.

Skip the main room and head straight to mine on the third floor.

Drink plenty of water today.

Carter

With a smile on my face, I take the box to my room to get ready. I take a quick shower to wash my workday away, and then do my hair and makeup before slipping on the dress and some heels.

I was right. When I turn in the mirror, I could see the bottom curve of my ass. I feel so sexy in this dress, and can't wait to see Carter tonight.

Once again, I put on a dress over this one because before I go to Club Red, I'm having dinner with my dad and Summer.

As I go out the door, I send a text to Carter.

Me: Thank you for the clothes. I'm wearing them under my dress to dinner with my dad and Summer tonight. See you after.

Carter: That's so much hotter than it should be. Until then, I'll be thinking of you.

Grabbing my purse, I head to Dad's house. Though I hesitate at the front door, remembering his conversation from last time. Since they are expecting me, I should walk right in, but I'm still hesitant. Thankfully, I'm saved from making the decision when the door opens, and Summer is standing there with a huge smile on her face. Then she laughs and pulls me in for a hug.

"I knew you'd be wrestling with the idea of whether to open the door or not."

Following her inside, the smell of Dad's pot roast fills the air.

Even though my dad could always throw something together, he really learned how to cook after my mom died. Sunday night dinners were a requirement no matter what I had going on.

As I walk in, Dad is setting the table, but he stops to give me a big hug.

"Get something to drink. Dinners ready," he says, as they place food on the table.

Sure enough, by the time I have my drink and I'm sitting at my spot at the table, everything is there and ready to go. Filling our plates, we talk and catch up on the week, what's been going on, and plans that are coming up.

"So, Summer says you've been spending quite a lot of time at Club Red," Dad says completely out of the blue.

I almost choke on the water that I was drinking.

"Knox!" Summer scolds him.

"Listen, this could be an uncomfortable subject, but I do know a lot of the people there. I want to make sure that who she is... seeing... is a good person."

That's my dad, always the protective one, even in the most awkward of circumstances.

"He's a good guy and the one that rescued me from Dustin the other night."

Once I got home, I called my dad and told him what had happened. I'm pretty sure Summer had to distract him in ways that I don't even want to know in order to stop him from going and killing Dustin himself. Probably the fact that Dustin spent several nights behind bars was a deterrent. But I know Dad's going to hire the best attorney to try to ensure that he stays behind bars for as long as possible.

"And his name is?" Dad asks.

I know he's not going to drop it.

Looking over at Summer, she shrugs her shoulders in an apology. We both know how my dad can get.

"His name is Carter," I tell him. Hoping that's enough to make him drop the subject.

"Carter what?"

"Jesus, Dad. Carter Morgan." The flash of recognition is instant in his eyes. Great.

" Is he treating you well?"

He asks in a way that makes me wonder if there's something I should know.

"Yes, why?"

"Just wondering, is all. He's the club owner, and there's always been this air of mystery about him."

Then I think about pressing and asking more questions. But I might have to answer questions that I don't necessarily want to right now, so I just let it go.

Thanks to Summer, we steer around to much safer topics. When it's time for me to leave, Summer asks to walk me out, saying she needs a girl talk moment. No sooner does the front door close behind us before she says what's on her mind.

"There's something you weren't saying at dinner. This Carter, he's the guy with the contract, right?"

"Yeah, he's also the guy who took me out on a date where he bought out the entire aquarium for us to have dinner alone. Even after saying no dates in the contract," I tell her. I wish I was exaggerating when I say her jaw hit the floor.

"So, the night after Dustin tries to attack you, he saves you. Then he takes you out to dinner, and not just any dinner, but a super fancy dinner. So this guy has money."

"Well, he's the owner of the club. So yeah. But I'm trying not to read too much into the dinner. I do have to get going, I'm supposed to meet him at the club tonight."

"Don't forget; I expect a phone call with some more juicy details. Now that I'm not living with Skye, I feel like I'm totally out of the loop." Summer pouts just a little before reaching in to give me another hug.

"We will have a girls' night soon."

"We'd better!"

I head to Club Red and park my car. Before I can even gather my stuff and step out of the car, two of the club's security guys that I've seen before are at my door, opening it. I just sit there stunned.

"Mr. Morgan's orders, we are to escort you to the door, ma'am," the one says.

Following them into the club, I check in, go to the lockers, and put my stuff away. When I step back into the lobby, the receptionist is standing there with a big smile on her face.

"This way. Mr. Morgan's orders are that you're to use the private elevator." She leads me down the hallway I just came out of, past the locker rooms, to a smaller elevator by some offices.

"There you go. Take it up to the third floor, and you know where his room is, right?"

"Yes, thank you."

I guess we are bypassing all the festivities downstairs today. Though I can't wait to see what he has planned upstairs. When I reach the door, it's closed. Hesitating for a moment before I take a deep breath and gently knock on the door. Carter opens it, and even though I've seen him in a suit many times, today, he steals my breath away.

He's removed the suit jacket, and the sleeves are rolled up on the button-down shirt that he wears.

"For as long as we are together, you don't ever have to knock on this door. This will be your room, too," he says, stepping aside.

"You know, I recently had the same conversation with my dad about knocking on the front door of the house. But in the end, it just doesn't feel like my home anymore, and it doesn't feel right to just burst on in," I tell him. I think he gets my meaning behind it.

This room doesn't feel like my room, so the chances that I will ever be comfortable walking right in are slim to none, but I appreciate the thought.

"You look stunning tonight," he says, his eyes drinking me in.

"You look handsome yourself," I say, taking a step toward him.

Closing the space between us, his lips land on mine before I can take my next breath. His hands cup my cheeks, and his kiss is gentle. It's completely out of character for our normal sessions.

Moving his hands gently into my hair, he deepens the kiss as he slowly backs me up and sets me on the bed. As he stands over me and looks at me one more time, his eyes soften. Then leaning in, he places a gentle kiss on my lips before standing up. Then the softness in his face is gone.

"Lay down in the center of the bed," he orders.

Once I do as he asks, he moves to one side and takes my hand in his.

He gently slides the paper-thin strap of my dress down my arm, pulling my arm out and placing the restraint attached to the bed around my wrist. Then he does the same to my other arm. My dress is still on, completely covering me except for my arms.

Carter stands beside the bed, staring at me. "I want to memorize you like this. You look like every guy's fantasy, and this is a memory I don't want to forget," he says softly.

I'm about to ask him what he means, but then he starts unbuttoning his shirt. At first, I'm scared to breathe, not wanting to break the spell. Beneath his shirt is an undershirt, and he hesitates. All I can do is encourage him with just my eyes. It must have worked because he rips the shirt off and stands there with the scars on full display.

To be honest, they're not as bad as I thought they would be. I was expecting something horrific based on how he kept talking about them. What I can see is raised scars and the parts of his skin that are slightly discolored.

But then he turns around, and the scars on his back are worse. But still, nothing that's going to send me running. Any woman that leaves because of them has serious issues.

The knife cuts slice across his back, causing some with raised skin and some are different colors of healed scars.

"If I wasn't tied to this bed, I would touch and kiss every one of those scars to remind you that they are a part of you. Further, they're proof that you fought hard and made it out alive. I don't understand how anyone can be disgusted with them. That just shows that there's something wrong with them, not you," I tell him.

At my words, I can see clearly the vulnerability in his eyes.

"I want to kiss you right now," I say.

Looking a little shocked at my words, he moves to me, and hesitantly, like he's still in shock at my words, he kisses me.

I try to put all the passion I can into that kiss without actually being able to touch him.

It's a slow and gentle kiss that sends warmth and love throughout my body. I can feel him relax as the kiss deepens. His lips move against mine like he's trying to tell me all his secrets without words, and I'm leaning into it with everything I have.

He slowly pulls away and glides his lips down my neck, and I can feel every single one of his kisses like they're a brand on my skin. His hands move up from my waist until he's cupping my face while his lips continue their journey down my body. Leisurely, he stops to suckle at the sensitive spots, making me quiver in anticipation as he moves lower. His hands run up and down my sides as his tongue traces circles around my belly button.

Moving away, he removes his pants, pulls out a condom, and slips it on. Then he helps turn me over on my hands and knees, twisting my hands with the restraints above my head.

He positions himself behind me, and I can feel the heat radiating off of him. His hands move to my hips, and he thrusts into me slowly at first, but then his movements become more intense as he moves faster and deeper. As he grips my hips tighter, I moan louder with each thrust.

With every movement, he's hitting all the right spots. I'm in pure bliss as he continues to move inside of me. Then his hand cups my breast, giving it a gentle squeeze as his other hand reaches down between us and rubs circles over my clit, sending sparks of pleasure throughout my body.

Every thrust brings me close and closer to an orgasm. Arching my back, I push harder against him as I reach the peak of pleasure before crashing back down onto the bed.

He lets out a loud groan himself before he gradually slows his movements until he stops completely. As we both catch our breath, he wraps his arms around me, holding me close.

Then he moves and unbinds my hands. I collapse on the bed, watching him put his shirt on. Even though he opened up and showed me the scars, I couldn't touch them. Nor did he let me look long.

Maybe he's regretting opening up in that way.

Chapter 18
Carter

"What is wrong with you?" Hunter says as I meet him in the hallway and go into our next meeting together.

"Nothing, why?"

"You're smiling, and it's scaring people. They're asking me if you're getting ready to fire a bunch of employees, and that's why you're so happy," Hunter says.

The fact that he's dead serious just makes me burst out laughing. "Is it that hard to believe I'm just happy?" I ask.

Hunter looks around the hallway, almost like he's looking for someone to back him up.

"You don't ever smile. It's kind of freaking me out. What is going on?"

Just the thought of why I'm so happy makes me even happier.

"I showed Gemma my scars, and she didn't run," I tell him.

His eyes go wide." I always told you the right woman wouldn't care about them. But the fact that you showed her. What brought that on?"

"After her ex attacked her in the parking lot, I took her out to dinner. She shared her story about the two of them. Feeling like I should share something about myself, I told her about my scars and my ex leaving. I don't know exactly what pushed me to do it. Maybe I was giving her a last chance to push me away. So last night, we came here to Club Red, and I showed her, and I think they turned her on more."

"Damn, it's about time. The great Carter Morgan is falling in love."

I stop dead in my tracks. "I didn't say anything about love," I say, my good mood instantly gone.

"You don't have to. It's written all over your face. One clue is that you're taking her on dates. You don't do that," he says as we continue walking down the hall.

"It's not love."

"Okay, whatever it is, enjoy it." He places a hand on my shoulder.

Damn, Hunter. Now I can barely focus on the meeting. It's an important one, as it's an update on all the issues with the virgin auction photo leak.

Cade opens the meeting, saying, "I've been working with marketing, and I think the best thing that we can do is launch a PR campaign. Right now, we need to try to drown out the press. That way, when you search Club Red online, the first things that pop up are not this photo leak or the articles surrounding it."

"What did you have in mind?" Hunter asks.

"It's been a while since we've made any public donations. I think maybe it's time to do a few of those," Cade says.

"What kind of public ones?" I ask.

Club Red always donates to different charities. Though we don't always make it a big public event. The founding members all put money in every month to split amongst the charities that we've agreed on.

"I think we focus on Oakside. They aren't local, so it'll send some reporters scrambling down there to do some stories and research. They'll shed light on a new charity that many people up here may not have heard of."

Oakside is the military rehabilitation center where some of our security guys have come from. They're based down in southern Georgia, just north of Savannah, and they don't get a lot of attention up here.

"I'm good with that," I nod.

"Good, because you might not like the next one," Cade says.

"What is it?" I ask, already annoyed that I have no idea what's coming.

"I think we need to humanize Club Red. Talk about how we donate to charities for single mothers. We can talk about how you grew up with a single mom," Cade says.

"No. Find a way to do it without putting me in the public spotlight. Hunter likes the spotlight. Use him," I grumble, shutting the idea down.

"No offense, but Hunter's happy home life doesn't make as great of a story. And while it's admirable that he's a single father who raised his son on his own, it doesn't pull at the heartstrings. Well, not quite as much as a single mom who's struggling to make ends meet versus the single billionaire dad," Gage says.

"And how do you know that? Do your books tell you, professor?" I shoot back. Though, I instantly felt bad about it.

"Look, I'm sorry. I just don't want to be in the spotlight. I never have been, and we've gotten this far without me having to put my face out there, along with my story. Outside of this room, I can count on one hand the number of people that know my background, and I would like to keep it that way. Would anyone of you put your history out there? With all your secrets that you've kept under wraps?"

Everyone in the room looks uncomfortable. Cade starts flipping through some papers in front of him. "We could highlight the charities and say that they were voted on by some of the members who were raised by single moms. We won't highlight any specific member," Cade says.

It's one thing to highlight the owners of a club, but we would never let out any private information about the members. Hell, the public doesn't even know who sits on our founding members' board. I'm going to keep it that way.

"Well," I say. "I was doing research on some of the other popular clubs in places like New York City and what they are doing. Then I got led down this rabbit hole. It's info that I thought you might find interesting. Did you know that there are thirty-five colleges here in the United States that have BDSM clubs that are recognized and funded by their university or college administration?"

That has everyone talking at once and asking a bunch of questions.

"Hang on, let me finish. I might be able to answer some of your questions. Here's a list of the universities. They include Harvard, Ohio State, Princeton, Stanford, Cornell, and the University of Chicago. On top of that, there are many more universities that don't have a dedicated club but regularly conduct workshops for students on safe BDSM practices. Beyond that, there are even several universities with professors who conduct research and offer classes that are included in the curriculum that covers BDSM."

"I know you're not putting this information out there without a plan," Troy, our club lawyer, says.

"The University of Chicago already has a registered club. One of their professors has done the research and published a book on the subject. I think we should partner with them to help with the classes they offer. Maybe include certain events where their club can come when the members aren't here. I think it would be beneficial to show that we're helping with the education of the community. But it could also entice some of these students to work towards membership here at the club," Cade says.

"Draft up a plan of how you want to go about this and present it at our next meeting. We will vote on it then," I say.

Everyone agrees, and after we cover a few small issues, I end the meeting and go to my office.

"You have a club member waiting to speak to you in your office." The security guy who was standing outside the door informs me.

"Great, the last thing I need is more issues that we need to deal with. What do you think the chances are that the member came to praise something good that we did?" I say to Hunter.

"I'll come in and sit with you since you're no longer in such a cheery mood," Hunter says.

But once he gets to the doorway of my office, we both stop in our tracks.

"I guess I don't need to be in this meeting after all. Good luck, brother," Hunter says, quickly exiting when he sees who is waiting.

It's Knox Gentry, Gemma's dad, sitting there.

After closing the door behind me, I take a seat at my desk. He moves from the couch to one of the chairs in front of me.

"Yesterday, I had dinner with my daughter, and she let it slip that she's been seeing you. To say I was shocked wouldn't even begin to cover it. So I figured that we need to talk," he starts.

"By all means," I say.

"When you've been a club member for a while, you start to know the members, what they like, their tastes, their habits. The fact that you keep everyone at bay with a contract is no secret. It's also no secret that you don't take a sub very often yourself, so knowing your current sub is my daughter gives me pause."

Well, at least he's not trying to bring up the fact that my fetish is not wanting to share myself with other people. I'm sure that's something he doesn't even want to think about with his daughter.

"Yes, we have a contract in place. A contract that states what her limits are and what my limits are. There's an NDA that's included. It states that she's not to talk about what happens in our dynamic to anyone who is not a Club Red member. As the owner of Club Red, I have to take extra precautions, not just to protect myself, but to protect the club and every member of it," I tell him honestly.

"Cut the bullshit. We both know that contract is to keep everyone at arm's length," he says without missing a beat.

I have to give him credit for being a straight shooter. Maybe once we get over this hump, I might like the guy.

"Listen, I just came out of a meeting where we have to work on PR for the club. It's very rare that we have an issue, but when we do, we need to be able to face it without the owners being under scrutiny."

"You mean the virgin auction photos leak? I read all about it. Is it a bigger problem that we all need to be worrying about?" He switches subjects.

"No, not yet. When I know, I will let the club know. Right now, it's more about burying the news story, so it's not the first thing you see when you search Club Red online. Now imagine pairing that news story with the owner of Club Red and there being previous scandals where my subs went and told the world what happened, what I was into, selling stories to the media for money. You've been around long enough to see clubs have lived and died by the reputation of their owners."

I can see the wheels turning in his head, but he doesn't say anything, so I continue.

"Now let's flip it. Heaven forbid anything ever got out about your daughter. That NDA covers her as well. I can't go speak out about her. The contract protects her. What's more, I'm happy to let you read it. Though with some exceptions, like the pages of her limits and mine and a few of her details blocked out. There are things no father should ever need to read. But that is contingent on getting her permission to let you do so."

"So essentially, what you two have is not taken outside of the club?"

I can tell he's starting to back down, but I'm going to be completely honest.

"We've had dinner outside the club a few times. What was talked about at those dinners is up to her to divulge. I don't have kids, and I can't imagine it's easy to know your daughter is involved in a club like this or that she's dating someone closer to your age than hers."

"I'm not worried about the age thing at all. Has she told you who I married?" Knox says, cracking a smile for the first time.

"Yes, her best friend. She has given me a bit of history on that. By the way, if you ever wonder if she is truly happy about the two of you. She gushes when she talks about you two."

That puts a genuine smile on his face. Though when he looks at me again, he almost looks sad.

"She's going to want more, and she's never going to be happy with you keeping her at a distance. I'm sure it works for now, especially after everything that happened with her ex. She's great at putting up a wall and trying to keep people at a distance. But it's just different when she's talking about you. That's what had me worried and feeling like I need to come down here to talk to you."

"Different, how?"

"After her mother died, she didn't let people in. Summer pushed her way in whether Gemma wanted it or not. Every day I'm grateful because, more than anything, Gemma needed a friend. In elementary, middle, and high school, there was just Gemma and Summer. She had no interest in making friends with anyone else. It wasn't until college that she slightly expanded her circle. But when she lets people in, she tends to hold on to them for dear life. I can tell she's letting you in, which means you have the biggest capacity of all to break her."

"We all have trust issues…" I start.

"It's not trust. She trusts people. Maybe sometimes more than she should. But she trusted you without knowing you. If you plan to stick around even for a while, you should hear the story of what happened from her. As her… "

He can't bring himself to say the word dom and the word boyfriend doesn't fit here.

"Anyway, as her whatever, you should know. And thank you for what you did in protecting her from Dustin." He stands to leave.

I stand too, and we both shake hands, and he leaves.

As I sit back down at my desk, I'm not going to lie. He has my curiosity piqued.

A quick Internet search brings up articles from the car accident, but that doesn't cover what Gemma went through and what she felt.

My mind whirled as I headed into my next meeting, debating if I wanted to pull her in closer or cut the strings now.

Chapter 19
Agent X

No matter how many years you worked for the department, your heart still races when you hear your name called to come talk to your boss.

"Sir?" I asked, stepping in and closing the door behind me.

"How soon can you have the information on Club Red that you've collected together to present?" He asks without even looking up from his desk.

"A few hours or so. Why?"

"Great, you have an hour to present it to my bosses. Get going."

With that, I know I am effectively dismissed.

I have no idea what it means that I'm presenting all of this. Hopefully, it means they will finally move forward on investigating the club. I spend the next hour putting all the information together so that it's readable and easier to understand than just my jumbled files and folders of everything. I know when my boss says present, that means on a slide show presentation. Thankfully, we use a template where I just have to plug stuff in instead of creating something from scratch.

"Ready?" my boss asks, coming up beside my desk.

"I guess. I better be." I hit save, put everything on the thumb drive, and take it with me as I follow my boss to the conference room.

They cover a few other things and updates in the meeting before my boss turns it over to me to present my findings on Club Red.

I go over all the information I have from the leak of the virgin auction photos, the information from my informants, and what has been said about Club Red in the past.

"You have no actual testimony from any of these women you claim that are complaining about the club, though?" One of the guys on my left asks.

I only know one of these guys by name. They're hardly ever in the office, but hopefully, they won't hold that against me.

"No. None of them have come forward to put an official testimony on the records. Due to the caliber of the members and the people associated with the club, we believe there have been threats and these women are fearing for their lives. As I said, the club does have mafia ties. It seems to be a neutral ground of sorts, but I'm sure that the families would go to any length to keep anyone quiet who wants to speak out."

"Do you have proof that they have mafia connections?" another man asks.

"After conducting stakeouts over the last couple of years, many known mafia family members have been in and out of the club on multiple occasions. As you can see from the photos in front of you."

"Do you have any leads on who leaked these auction photos and their motive behind it? Why they didn't just go to the police? Or did they decide to sell the story for money?" The guy in the gray suit to my right asks.

"No, the identity of the photographer is being kept under wraps. It's heavily guarded. Apparently, because they are currently a club member. There's also a reward put out via the Chicago underground for the identity of that person. The photo leaker is in very high demand. My guess is to make sure they stay quiet."

"And you know this how?" my boss asks.

"From several informants that I use who keep me up to date on what is being said and what is going on."

These guys have all worked their way up the ladder, so they know not to even ask about my informants because I will protect them to my deathbed. If it gets out that a cop is snitching on their informants, it's pretty much signing your death warrant. Not just for you but for your informants too.

The guy in the grey suit looks at me, saying, "We're going to be very upfront with you, son. We have put in a lot of work on this over the years, so we want you on our team. The problem is, you know as well as we do if we were to take what we have right now into a court of law, we would be laughed out. We have nothing that will get us a warrant to search the building or anything that will force them to hand over their client list.

Furthermore, we can't even go after anyone associated with this auction because the person who's selling it is calling it a 'virgin auction,' whereas the club was calling it 'spending time with a virgin.' Selling someone's virginity and spending time with a virgin are two completely different things, especially in the eyes of the law."

"Now that we know mafia members have been in and out of this club, it's of interest. If they're associated with the mafia in any way, that could be our ticket to taking them down. The problem is especially here in Chicago, the city is becoming very sex-positive, and BDSM does not have the same negative connotation that it used to. There are classes on it at universities; there are clubs about it attached to different schools, professors are writing books about it, there's an entire social media website dedicated to it and the learning and teaching of it."

My boss chimes in. "What I'm trying to say is that the police and the government are all going to tread lightly because this is a large voter group and a big enough community that if they were to rally...

Well, we don't know if it has the type of power to affect an election because most of these people choose to stay so far underground. Who knows what they'll do, as the community has never been attacked like this before. So, before we make any claims or make any moves, there needs to be undisputable evidence of wrongdoing. Either women or children being hurt, or a mafia connection."

"That's where you come in," Mr. Gray Suit says. "We want you to focus part of your energy on this. Yes, it needs to be in your downtime, but we are willing to offer you more resources and help by doing some of the digging. It needs to be kept quiet, and you need to not raise any suspicions about it, or we will deny everything and say that you are going rogue and acting on your own."

This is what I've been waiting for, the opening to move forward against the club.

"Why is this so important to you?" One of the men in the back who hasn't spoken before asks.

Because I don't want to lose their faith in me, I must choose my words very carefully. I make a split-second decision to beef up the truth. My gut is telling me that this is needed.

"I know a woman who was sucked into the club, brainwashed and has had some horrible things happen to her. She's terrified to speak out, and I can't force her to, but I know there are others there too.

Lord only knows what they are doing to these girls. If I can help her by going about it another way, I will do everything in my power to do so."

There's some whispering around the table, and everyone looks around. What catches my attention is the look from my boss. This is the first time he's heard about all this, and I'm sure he's wondering why I didn't bring it up to him beforehand. But really, he's always been one of those; if someone isn't willing to help themselves, there's not much we can do about it, people.

"If there's any way you can get this woman to speak, even if it's an anonymous statement, it would help the case greatly. But let's move forward quietly and slowly," Mr. Gray Suit says.

"What about getting someone in there undercover as a member?" I ask. Because that's something I've been wanting to do for a while, but I had no one to back me on it.

"I've looked over their membership policies and the extensive background checks. Not to mention the fact that you have to be referred by another member. Right now, it would be using too many resources. But if we gather some more evidence and it warrants putting more time into it, we can come back to it," Mr. Gray Suit says.

Then he stands, effectively dismissing the meeting.

I collect my stuff, and eventually, it is my boss and I left it in the conference room.

"Is this woman you're talking about, is it anyone I know?" he asks.

I stare into his eyes, unwilling to lie to him but also unwilling to admit the truth.

He nods his head and doesn't push the issue.

"Alright, let's take these bastards down."

Chapter 20
Gemma

Finally, I'm finished wrapping up a big project, making the custom engagement ring. He liked my first draft but needed several changes, and it took four versions before we got it right. Not the most revisions ever needed, but pretty close. I just finished with the ring, and he will be coming on Monday morning to see it. After putting it and a few other projects I'm working on back in the safe, I make sure everything is locked up before closing up my workspace.

The shop itself doesn't close for a few more hours, but I don't let anyone mess around in my office. So I'm always the one to close and lock it before leaving. I'm excited about going home and getting changed. Later tonight, I'm supposed to meet up with Carter at Club Red. But first, I'm having dinner with Skye, who says she's been missing me and wants to catch up, so she's bribing me with takeout from my favorite fried chicken place.

Me: I'm leaving now.

Skye: Perfect, I just picked up the food and will be there right before you!

When I say goodbye to my coworkers still in the shop, I find Dustin standing at the checkout counter. I freeze in place. Even though my coworker has no idea about my personal life, she is more than happy to talk to him.

"Here she is now. Gemma, this lovely gentleman was asking for you." The girl, who can't be more than the minimum twenty-one-year-old required for this job, says, trying to flirt with him.

"What are you doing here? How did you even get out of jail?" I snap at him. My coworker's eyes go wide as she slowly backs up to one of the several silent alarm buttons we have scattered around.

"I have my ways. You didn't think the cops would hold me, did you?" he says. Though he sounds absolutely nothing like himself, at least the part of him, I was allowed to know.

While I keep Dustin's attention on me, the girl reaches and presses the alarm button.

"Who are you? This is not the guy I dated. Is your ego this bruised because I dumped you?" I ask, not quite sure what has gotten into his head.

He lets out this almost manic laugh that I don't understand.

"You just never took the time to get to know the real me. Everything was going great, and then you had to dump me. If you hadn't caused any waves, everything would have been over a few months after the wedding. Then you could have gone back to your nice, normal little life."

What in the hell is he talking about? Then something my dad has drilled into me comes to mind. My father has money, a lot of it. He always warned me about people wanting to be my friend or even date me because of it. That's exactly what it sounds like right now.

"This is about my dad's money, isn't it?"

"Well, she catches on quick," he looks over at the other girl, giving her a flirty wink and a smile like he's not some psychopath.

"My plan couldn't have gone any better with how well you got along with my family. That was one thing I hadn't expected. But all you had to do was marry me. Once we were married, we get your dad to pay off my debts. Then we'd get us a nice little nest egg, file for divorce, and split it."

"You didn't think this out very well, did you? There was never going to be a marriage or a wedding without a prenup. My dad wouldn't have allowed it, and he wouldn't give us a cent without one."

At this point, I can tell he's getting irritated. It's apparent that it never occurred to him there would be a prenup because what do I have that we need a prenup for? Right now, everything would have come after the wedding. But if you don't grow up with money, you don't think about things like protecting it.

As he opens his mouth to speak, the door bursts open.

Damn, the cops got here really fast. But no words are spoken as two people in suits tackle Dustin to the ground. The next thing I know, Carter's arms are around me.

"You okay, baby girl?" He asks me while backing me away from Dustin.

"Yeah, how did you get here before the cops?"

"After he attacked you the last time, I've had security following you. As soon as he showed up, they called me. I was having lunch with a client a few blocks away. Are you sure you're all right?" he asks again.

I nod just as the cops pull up. We spend the next thirty minutes giving statements about what happened. We show them the security footage, and they pull up case records that were started when he attacked me in the parking lot of Club Red. Though the police don't seem surprised that he got out of jail, they haul him in. But I have no faith that this time he's going to stay there.

When I go back inside, my phone is ringing. While I was talking to the police, I heard it go off several times.

"It's probably Skye. We were supposed to meet for dinner," I say, picking up the phone.

"Skye..."

"Where the hell are you? If you were going to stop somewhere, you should have said something. Why didn't you pick up your phone?"

"I..." I have no words, and thankfully, Carter seems to realize that, so he takes the phone from my hand. With the other hand, he takes mine and guides me to sit down.

"Skye, it's Carter. Dustin showed up at her work. Calm down; he's already been taken off in cuffs. I had a security guy following her and was having lunch a few blocks away. I got here just before the cops did. She says she's fine, but I think it's starting to hit her about what happened. I'm going to take her back to my place, feed her, and make sure that she's okay. Do you need anything? Yes, I promise to keep you updated. I'm going to have one of my guys drive her car home. He'll knock on the door and hand you her keys. Yes, the same one as before." He hangs up the phone as my boss walks in the door.

"Gemma, what happened?" he asks.

Instantly, Carter stands between us.

"Who the hell are you?" My boss asks, stopping in his tracks.

"That's my question to you," Carter says.

That's when I stand, putting my hand on his arm. "This is my boss. He owns the place."

Carter leads me to a chair. Then once again, he explains what happened to my boss, saving me the trouble. My boss ends up shooing me out with Carter.

After that, things become a blur as Carter takes control. He gathers my stuff, deals with whoever is still there, and with my car.

"Wake up, sweetheart," Carter's gentle voice says, pushing hair out of my face.

Opening my eyes, I see that the car is parked in some kind of garage. I'm a little surprised as I don't even remember falling asleep.

"I'm sorry I fell asleep on you," I say, sitting up and running a hand through my hair.

"Perfectly understandable. With what just happened, I figured I'd let you get a little nap, but I also figured it wouldn't be a good idea for my doorman to see me carrying an unconscious woman. He's never seen a woman go up to my apartment," he chuckles.

I force a smile.

His driver gathers my stuff, and Carter focuses on getting me out of the car and helping me into the building. Once we are in his apartment, which is the penthouse, on the top floor, he sits me down on the couch.

"Do you ever worry about there being a fire, and they shut down the elevators, and you're on the top floor?" I ask. It's the first thing that comes to my mind.

At my words, he stops what he's doing and looks over at me.

"We have a security plan in place, and we do emergency drills. I'm as prepared as I can be." He says while going into the kitchen and coming back with a glass of water.

"Drink. Are you in the mood for anything in particular for dinner?"

"Don't laugh. But some deep-dish pizza sounds really good right now."

"Why would I laugh? That you're hungry is a good sign," he says, opening one of the kitchen drawers.

"There's a place a block over that has great pizza. I can place an order, and one of my men will go get it. What do you like on your pizza?"

"Green peppers and black olives."

Shaking his head, he looks at me for a moment before pulling his phone out to place the order.

I take in his place because I never thought I would be here with the contract in place. My guess is I probably won't be back, so I'll take any chance to learn what I can about Carter.

The room is set up to take advantage of the view. On the wall next to the windows are some bookcases with beautiful leather-bound books. There are some picture frames of a slightly younger Carter and what looks to be his mom.

In addition, there's also a picture of him and a guy his age in military uniform with what looks like a desert behind them.

"That's Hunter. He's my best friend. We met in boot camp and started the club together. You'll see him around at some point. I'm sure he's at the club more than I am," Carter says, walking up behind me.

"Is that your mom?" I point to the picture I saw first.

"Yep, that was taken right before I left for deployment. The one where I got injured."

"Was Hunter one of the men with you when you were injured?" The question seems to catch him off guard.

"No, he was stationed with a different unit. But by some dumb luck during that deployment, we happened to get stationed in the same place. But no, he wasn't with me when I was injured."

"Pizza is here," he says when the doorbell rings. Then, kissing the top of my head, he walks towards the door.

I don't even bother to get up because I know whatever it is, Carter will take care of it.

"The food is here, so I'm going to set the table. While I do that, you need to call your dad."

Going to my purse, I pull out my phone. Then shoot Skye a quick text quick.

Me: Made it to Carter's place. Will talk to you later.

Then I call my dad.

"Hey, Gemma, what's up?" he asks. Obviously, no one has called him yet.

"Hi, Dad. I expected Skye to call you and tell you what was going on or call in a fit of panic when I didn't answer her phone call."

"What happened?" His voice changes, instantly getting serious.

"Is she okay?" I hear Summer ask in the background.

"Summer is here. Let me put you on speakerphone." The sound changes slightly when he speaks again.

I recap yet again what happened with Dustin at work. Then I tell them about Carter showing up, Skye's multiple phone calls, all leading up to how I am currently at Carter's apartment.

"You're sure you're all right? We can come and get you anytime. You just say when," Summer says.

"I promise I'm okay. Carter just ordered food, so I think I'm going to hang out here."

"Put Carter on the phone," Dad says in his serious business voice.

Hesitating for a moment, I look over at Carter.

"My dad wants to talk to you," I tell him.

Nodding, he walks over, takes the phone from me, and sits me down at the table, putting a slice of pizza on my plate.

"I'll talk to him. You eat," he says, taking my phone and going into the kitchen to finish whatever it was he was doing.

Since I can't hear what's being said, I pick up my pizza and take a bite. It's really good pizza. A few minutes later, Carter walks back in and hands me my phone again, placing another kiss on the top of my head before walking off.

"Hello?" I say when my dad answers. He's much calmer.

"It sounds like you're in good hands there, but you let me handle Dustin this time. Carter and I have a plan. Get some rest and call us in the morning."

"Okay, Dad. I love you."

"I love you too, sweetie."

"Tell Summer I love her too and give her a big hug for me."

"Will do. Get some rest."

When I hang up, Carter joins me at the table. He's made a salad and has set more water in front of me.

"What's this plan you and my dad have for Dustin?" I ask.

He hesitates for only a moment.

"We're not sure how he was able to get out of prison so fast. But we're going to have one of our founding members, Mase, get involved to find out why. Then we're going to make sure it doesn't happen again and put the living fear of God into him," he says.

"Who is Mase?" I ask.

"He's a very well-connected guy in the city,"

His answer is kind of vague. I get a feeling it's one of those don't ask don't tell sort of things, so I decide to drop the subject. As we finish eating, we don't speak much. But he watches every move I make and gets up and refills my water without me even having to ask. As soon as I finish the first piece of pizza, he puts another piece of pizza on my plate.

"Come on. Let me give you a tour of the place." He takes my hand after dinner and shows me around. There are four bedrooms, plus an office. What I'm excited to see is a movie room.

It's everything I would expect from a top-floor penthouse apartment. The place is neat and tidy, and you can tell he has someone in here regularly to clean. Everything has a place and everything is in its place.

He takes me into his bedroom, and it's decorated in shades of blue and grey with a massive bed in the center.

When I turn around to look at him, he wraps an arm around my waist and pulls me in close for a kiss. He presses his lips gently against mine, and I feel my heart flutter as he wraps his arms around me and deepens the kiss. We stand there for what feels like an eternity until he pulls away, still holding me close.

He leads me to the bed, kneeling in front of me to remove my shoes. Taking my hand, he undresses me. When his fingers brush against my skin, it sends tingles throughout my body. Then, he lays me down on the bed, pulling the covers over me before giving me one last kiss on the forehead and turning off the light.

The moonlight is streaming through the window, and as Carter moves to his side of the bed and removes his clothes, I can see some of the scars on his back. He notices me looking and turns around with a sad smile on his face.

"You don't have to hide them, you know," I say tenderly.

"Old habits die hard," he says, climbing into bed.

He pulls me to him, and I snuggle up against him. We kiss, his lips are soft and gentle against mine as my hands roam over his body, tracing the lines of scars that tell a story of pain and suffering.

Slowly, I trace each scar on his chest with my fingertips, kissing them lightly as I go. He holds me close, and I can feel his heart beating against mine. I rest my head on his chest and close my eyes, listening to the sound of his breathing, feeling safe in his embrace.

Once I trace the last one, he rolls me over and kisses me with such passion. His hands move over my body as he kisses me all over, from my neck to my stomach. I'm lost in the feeling of his lips and hands on me. I'm taken away by how alive I feel and how free I am in his arms.

Being able to touch him makes the sensations ten times more intense than having my hands bound to the bed. He kisses his way up my body until he reaches my lips, and I can feel myself wanting more. Then, moving his body over mine, he looks deep into my eyes.

He enters me slowly, and the sensation of no condom for the first time steals my breath away. This is different than the times at the club. Those felt like sex, and this feels like making love. The distinct difference makes it more intense.

He keeps his eyes on mine the whole time. It's as if our souls are connecting, not just our bodies.

Our movements become more urgent, and my body is trembling with pleasure. As we move together in an ever-increasing rhythm, our eyes stay locked in a passionate gaze.

My orgasm is building and I'm trying to hold it back, wanting this moment to last forever. Sensing my hesitation, he moves his hand to my clit, gently rubbing it as he increases the pace of his thrusts.

The pleasure is overwhelming, and I let out a loud moan as I cum, my body shaking with pleasure.

He follows me over the edge, and I feel his body tense up as he cums deep inside me. Afterward, we lie there for a few moments, still wrapped in each other's embrace.

For hours, we lie there talking about our lives, sharing secrets and stories until we both drift off to sleep.

"Gemma, wake up!" I hear Carter saying a little panicked

I jolt up. I was just in the car with my mom. We were laughing and singing her favorite song. Then the crunching of metal and her screams are still bouncing in my head.

Curling up in a ball, I cover my ears, trying to get rid of the sound. Strong hands cover mine, and when I open my eyes, Carter is looking at me. Even though his mouth is moving, I hear nothing. Then a moment of blissful silence before it hits me, I'm at his house, in his bed, and I hear him again.

"Talk to me," he says, trying to get my attention.

"I'm fine," I say, sitting up.

The first signs of morning light are creeping through the window, and suddenly, all I have is an urge to get home. So, I stand up, find my clothes on the floor and begin to get dressed.

"What are you doing? Sit down and talk to me," he says, slipping his boxers back on.

"What do you want to talk about? I had a nightmare that I haven't had in years, and I have no idea what triggered it. But all I want is my bed and my own space so that I can figure out what caused it."

"Well, let's get you dressed. Sit for a minute, calm down, and I'll arrange for you to get home."

"I don't want to stay here. Right now, I don't feel comfortable here. I want to go. I'll catch a cab."

"Like hell, you will. My driver will take you home. Just give me a minute to call him. He has an apartment a few floors down."

I go to the bathroom, and by the time I come out, he's dressed. His driver is standing by his front door, so I rush out, not looking back. All I can think about is getting home safely.

For some time, I've been so good at not triggering these nightmares. Something slipped last night, and I need to make sure I don't ever do it again.

Chapter 21

Carter

Since she ran out of my house the other day, I haven't heard from Gemma. I've been trying so hard to give her space, but I'm going crazy. If I didn't have a security guard posted at her apartment, I wouldn't have been able to give her this much time. But today, waking up and still not having heard from her, I can't take it anymore.

After I got a few things done at work, I waited until the respectable time of nine o'clock in the morning before making my way to her place. I know she didn't go to work yesterday, and she hasn't left for work today. And I intend to at least find out why.

"Is she okay?" I ask, skipping all the pleasantries.

Skye looks me up and down before she speaks.

"I don't know. What has she told you?"

"Can I come in?" I ask.

"Not until you answer my question."

"She hasn't told me anything. We had the night together where I thought we connected on a deeper level. I took her to my place which, by the way, I never take people there. She had a nightmare, ran out early in the morning, and I haven't heard from her since."

"Well, that's more information than I had before she got home, locked herself in her room, and hasn't come out. Though she eats what I bring her. But that's about it. If she didn't get out of her room today, I was going to call Summer and her dad." She steps aside to let me in.

"Let me try. That might still be an option we can take. Which one is her room?"

"Last door on the left." Skye points towards the hallway. "Listen, I have to go to class and then I have to work after that. Regardless of what she says, will you please stay here with her until I get back? I don't want her here alone."

"I promise to be here when you get back. Can you leave her dad's number and your number on the refrigerator in case I need them?"

"Yep, I'll leave Summer's too. Maybe try Summer before you call her dad."

"Do you know if she's called into work?" I ask. My mind is racing with how I can help her.

"I called yesterday, and they told her to take the week off after what happened."

"Okay, perfect. Get going. I promise I'll take care of her."

Walking down the hallway, I knock lightly on her door. But no sound comes from the other side.

"Sweetheart, can I come in?" I ask, hearing no noise.

Needing to have eyes on her to make sure she's okay, I test the doorknob and find it unlocked. So opening the door, I find her lying in bed with her hair a mess and blankets pulled up to her chin. It's obvious she has been crying.

"Go away, Carter," she says, pulling the blanket over her head.

"Not a chance, sweetheart," I say. Then I slip out of my clothes, place them on top of the dresser, and slide into bed with her.

Holding her tight against me, I just let her be. I don't talk or force questions. Instead, I let her know that I'm here for her. Hopefully, she'll feel safe knowing that I'm not going anywhere.

We simply lie together peacefully. At some point my phone dings, but I ignore it. For a while, she drifts in and out of sleep, but then she finally begins to speak.

"Today's the anniversary of my mom's death. That night at your house, I had the nightmare of her dying. It's one I haven't had in years, and it took a lot of therapy to stop having that dream.

When my mom had the accident and died, I was in the car. Though I was in a car seat in the back and that car seat saved my life."

I kiss the top of her head but don't push her for anything else. My hope is that maybe she'll want to share more with me.

"We were out on a mommy-daughter date, getting school clothes for me. My dad insisted we get our nails done, and I remember how happy my mom was. This is right about the time Dad started making money, so he was always spoiling us. The weather was nice all day, and we were singing songs in the car, laughing, joking, and having a good time."

Turning in my arms, she faces me, resting her head on my shoulder. Though she's not looking at me, she puts her hand on my chest and traces my scars. It takes everything in me to concentrate on what she says after that.

"On the way home, it started to rain. But it wasn't too bad. After Mom turned the radio down, we were planning what I was going to wear the first day of school, choosing from the clothes that we had bought.

The next thing I remember is how Mom's screams filled the air. There were sounds of crunching metal and I felt like I was flying, even though I was confined in my car seat. I had never been so scared in my entire life.

To this day, Mom's screams still haunt me. Watching blood drip down her face and her life leaving her was horrifying. It seemed forever until the rescue teams could get there to help us. And that's my nightmare. Reliving over and over and over again every night for months. Then suddenly the other night at your house."

"Oh, sweetheart, I'm sorry you had to deal with that," I say, at a loss for words.

"Many years later, Dad told me he and my mom had argued about whether I needed to still be in a car seat. But Mom said she felt I needed the extra protection above and beyond what the law required. They had had several arguments about it, but in the end, Dad said the car seat saved my life.

Growing up, my dad was a great dad, and he still is. He busted his butt to make a good life for me. I never saw him date. Now, he's one of my best friends. When I found out about him and Summer, I was a little upset, but I wanted him happy. After raising me, and everything he's been through, he deserves to be happy.

Night after night, when I had my nightmares, he sat up with me. Sometimes he would let me sleep in bed with him because I was terrified of being alone. Even though he was grieving himself, he helped me through grief counseling."

"It's because he loves you and even now, he's going to protect you. Look what he was doing with Dustin. He's still protecting you."

"I don't want him to know that the nightmares are back. Summer just married him, and I want him to enjoy his life and concentrate on that. I'm an adult and I can work through it myself this time."

Not wanting to make a promise I can't keep, I think about my next words very carefully.

"I'll make you a deal. I won't tell your dad so long as you don't fall off the face of the Earth like this again. You've got to at least check in, even if you're having a bad day and tell me. You're allowed to have bad days, but I have to know that you're okay and not just disappearing on me for days on end."

"Okay, I can do that," she says, yawning.

My guess is if she's still having nightmares, she hasn't been sleeping very well.

"You've been having the nightmares since the night at my place?"

"Every night."

"Well, get some sleep. I'm right here and I'm not going anywhere."

It's not long before she's asleep. After slipping out of bed, I put my jeans back on and go out to the main area of her apartment. Skye has been taking care of her and she deserves some downtime.

With Gemma asleep, I pick up the apartment, wash some dishes, and clean the bathroom. Then I start a load of laundry. For now, just the towels.

I decide to let her sleep the best she can. When she sleeps right through lunch, I answer some emails on my phone and then start dinner. Though it's a bit early, I figure since she missed lunch she will be hungry. When the food is ready, I set the table and then I head into her room.

Sitting down on the bed next to her, I gently rub her arm.

"Sweetheart, you have got to get up and eat something."

Grumbling, she turns over on her back and cracks an eye open to look at me.

"How long have I been asleep?"

"Over six hours. You slept through lunch, so I made dinner a bit early."

"You made dinner?"

"Don't sound so shocked. I know how to cook. Come on, get up." I slap her thigh playfully, but then go back to the kitchen to give her some privacy to get up and move. A few minutes later, she joins me.

"What is this?" she asks, sitting down in the chair that I hold out for her.

"Chicken parmesan, a salad, and of course, your water, since you have been asleep for so long."

"We have the stuff to make chicken parmesan?" she asks, filling up her plate.

"Yep, now you eat."

Even though she starts eating, she looks around the house.

"Did you clean too?"

"Yes. And if you were going to ask, yes, I know how to clean. Just because I don't like to do it and I prefer to hire someone for my daily cleaning, doesn't mean I don't know how. The same with cooking. But my girl needed to be taken care of, so I have no problems with it."

Her eyes shoot to mine the moment I say, my girl. I wait for questions, but they don't come. Hopefully, it feels right to her because saying it felt right to me.

"I appreciate you sharing the story of what happened with your mom," I say. I want her to know that I know it wasn't easy to talk about.

"My therapist says I have security issues and issues with feeling safe. Sometimes it looks like trust issues, but it's just me needing to control a situation and feel in control of it."

"I get that. Honestly, that's a huge part of the reason I do the contract. To help you feel safe while making me feel safer, too."

When she gives me a forced smile, I want to make her understand.

"It's my job to make you feel safe, not just in the bedroom or at the club. If you need extra security to feel safe, tell me I'll make it happen. If you need to set more boundaries, then let's do it. Just say the word."

While I don't like the idea of more boundaries or her putting up walls between us, if that's what she needs, then so be it. My phone goes off on the counter, but I ignore it.

"You're not going to get that?"

"No, it can wait. I'm having dinner with you. Right now, you have my attention because you are what's important."

She looks down at her plate, but it doesn't hide the cute blush that covers her face.

After dinner, we mostly discuss her favorite foods, movies, TV shows, and other small talk. Then she gets up to do the dishes.

"Hey, let me do these. Why don't you go take a nice relaxing bath?"

"But you cooked, so I should clean."

"Not today, baby girl. Go take a bath and relax. I've got this."

Hesitating for a moment, she nods, leans in, and kisses my cheek before scampering off to her room to get ready for a bath. Once she's in the bathroom with the water running, I check my phone to see I have a missed call from Mase. We don't talk much outside the club, but I did ask for his help with the whole Dustin situation. He was more than happy to help. I think he might have enjoyed it more than he wants to admit.

"Sorry, I was making sure Gemma ate dinner," I tell him when I call him back.

"It's nothing that won't keep. I just wanted to let you know that the whole Dustin situation has been taken care of. Those that let him out early have been dealt with, and Dustin has been... talked to. Dustin will be taking another job in New York City and has been warned that if he steps foot in Chicago again for any reason, he won't be leaving it." Mace says with a hint of amusement in his voice.

"Did you make him suffer?" Normally I'd wish someone mercy in Mace's hands, but he went after my girl. That I'm not willing to forgive so quickly.

"Oh yes. He cried like a baby. Tried to reason with me that he has a family he wants to come back to visit. I reminded him that they could always visit him. Though he tried to get out of it with every trick in the book. Actually, it was quite pathetic. But now the poor boy has a few extra scars that he can lie to the next girl about getting. I also called in a favor from a buddy in New York City to keep an eye on him and make sure he has some really bad luck in the city. He's going to become a plaything."

"Good. So long as he doesn't bother Gemma again. I appreciate this."

"Don't worry about it. I owe you much more than this, so I'm happy to start repaying some of the debt. If you need me to take care of anyone else, just say the word. This was pretty fun."

We hang up, and I pour a glass of wine and take it into the bathroom for Gemma, who is relaxing in a bath. A bath, I would love nothing more than to join her in, but today is not the day for that.

"What do you say tomorrow you and I get out of the house? Skye said you have the rest of the week off of work. I think you should enjoy it."

"What did you have in mind?"

Chapter 22

Gemma

Carter hasn't left my side for the last few days. With my time off of work, he took me out so that we could enjoy the city as tourists. Something that we locals very rarely got a chance to do. We took a boat down the river and went to the aquarium during regular business hours.

We visited a couple of museums and tried a few restaurants that we had been wanting to try. Of course, the restaurants I picked out had more burgers and fries, and his were fancy steak dinners, but we balanced each other out well.

He didn't leave my side. After stopping by his place so that he could pack a bag, he came and stayed at my place all week. Today he has brought me to Club Red and has me sitting at the bar while he goes and checks in. Since he hasn't been here all week, he wants to make sure there's nothing he's needed for in his office.

Jax, the bartender, is keeping an eye on me per Carter's request. As I'm sitting there looking out over what's happening with the club tonight, a beautiful fake blonde walks up. You know the kind. One that doesn't look like a single thing about her is real. Her hair color is from a bottle, her lips injected with something, she's had a boob job, and even her tan looks fake in this light. Nonetheless, she still looks gorgeous.

"So, you are Carter's new plaything?" she asks.

I have no clue how to answer, but that doesn't stop her from speaking.

"He'll get bored with you and come back to me. He always does. Don't get too attached; it just makes things more difficult." Then she turns around and walks off, quickly disappearing into the voyeur hall.

All I can do is sit there completely shell-shocked.

"What did that blonde have to say to you?" Carter walks up beside me, and he's glaring in the direction where she walked off.

"Were you ever together with her like you are with me?" I ask, stumbling over my words.

"For a while, yes, a very brief time. She was one of my subs with a contract. I quickly found out she is an ugly person on the inside, and I couldn't stand to be around her. Why, what did she say?"

When I tell him, he glares again in the direction she went.

"It's against Club Red rules for past subs to harass the current sub. I never liked her attitude and had plans to revoke her membership when we broke things off. But another dom wanted to play with her, so that's the only reason we've kept her around. I will remind them that she is breaking the rules, and if she continues, I will revoke both of their memberships. Wait here." He kisses my temple and goes back in the direction that he came from.

I see one of the guys that I know is security, but tonight he's in plain clothes walking in the direction that the blonde went. A few minutes later, she's walking out beside him, not looking very happy. She glares in my direction, and I can't help but smile and offer her a little wave as she's escorted out of the club.

I've never been a very petty person, but the satisfaction of seeing her thrown out made me extremely happy.

"You are beautiful when you smile." A man I've never seen before says as he sits down on the barstool next to me.

I glance behind him at Jax, who catches my eye and seems to understand.

"I'm sorry, but I'm not interested. I'm waiting on my dom." It's what Carter has told me to tell other men if they approach me while I'm here.

"Well, he's not here, and no dom worth his salt would leave a girl like you unattended. I could show you what the real Club Red is." He says, reaching out, trying to touch my arm, but I move out of his way.

"Red," I say loudly to grab anyone's attention who is nearby. But he ignores me and touches my arm anyway.

"Stop. Red means stop. I've heard her tell you no from across the bar," Jax says, stepping up to me.

"Mind your own business, bartender. This is between club members. She doesn't mean it." Instantly panic grips me, and I glance again at Jax.

"So, you have a contact with her and talked about this scene before tonight? Because I know she has a contract with another dom. One you don't want to mess with," Jax says.

Then, winking at me, he glances behind me. When I turn to look, the bubble of safety comes back.

"Carter," I sigh.

"Your girl told him no, used Red, and he didn't want to take no for an answer," Jax fills Carter in.

"Jesus, you're a trouble magnet tonight. Aren't you, sweetheart?" Carter says. Then he flags down the same guy who just threw the blonde out.

"Have this guy removed and his membership revoked for violation of the consent and red rule," he tells Security.

"I didn't violate any rules. She wanted it," the jerk says.

"I told you no, said red, and said that I was waiting on my dom. I believe your exact words were no dom worth his salt would leave his girl unattended." I stand up for myself.

"That's what I heard as well. Should we pull up the security footage?" Jax points to three different cameras that would have caught the entire event.

When the guy doesn't move, Security forcefully moves him out of the room and into the lobby to take care of revoking his membership.

"I can't take my eyes off of you today. Can I?" Carter says. But there's a smile in his eyes that lets me know he's ready to play. "

"Are you okay?" His eyes roam over me.

"Yep, thanks to you and Jax. Thank you, by the way," I say, turning to Jax.

"No problem. I'm here anytime you need me."

"Well, I appreciate it, and your next paycheck will show you just how much," Carter says.

"I'll always protect the girls here, but I sure as hell won't say no to that either, Carter."

I don't miss that they're on a first name basis with each other, and I feel like there's a story there.

Carter takes my hand and leads me up to the second floor, where the themed rooms are. I've yet to be here, but Skye has told me a lot about them.

"Have you been up here to look around at the different themed rooms?" Carter asks.

"No, I haven't."

Once we get to the top of the stairs, there's a much smaller lounge area, like the area with the couch downstairs. It overlooks the bar area. We continue walking down a long hallway with rooms on either side.

"The rooms on the right are the different themed rooms, and the ones on the left can be rented out by members for the night. If they're open, then you're free to come and go in them as you wish. Sometimes people will rent them out but keep the window next to the door open so that you can watch. Or possibly, they'll keep the door open and invite you in," Carter explains.

As we walk down the hall, I peek into a few of the themed rooms. One looks like a doctor's office, another one like a classroom, there's a room where everything is red, and then another one that has mirrors for walls.

We stop at the end of the hallway, and in front of us is a door. When we enter the room, everything is in gold. In the center is a platform with several steps leading up to a large ornate throne. One of the security guys has been standing there, and I'm guessing Carter has him there to reserve our spot because as soon as he walks up with me, Security moves out of the way.

Carter takes a seat on the throne and sits me on his lap like he would downstairs, with my back to his chest and my legs spread over his. Again, per his request, I'm not wearing any underwear under my dress. So when it rides up, anyone in the room can see me on full display.

Reaching a hand around me, he plays with me as a few couples stop to watch.

"Pull your dress down and show off those amazing tits. Give them a good show," he orders.

Doing as he asks, I pull down the top of my dress, exposing my breasts to everyone in the room. He plays with them, lightly tracing circles around my nipples, then pinches my nipples and tugs on them until they're hard. I can feel his other hand between my legs as he fingers me slowly at first but then increases the speed as I moan louder.

"I want you to cum for everyone here to see," he whispers into my ear.

Then he increases the pressure and speed of his fingers until I'm panting and moaning loudly, with my body writhing against his. Just as I'm about to reach my peak, he slows down suddenly, leaving me hanging on the edge of pleasure. After repeating this several times, until finally, I can't take it anymore. With one last thrust of his fingers, I scream out in pleasure as the wave of my orgasm crashes over me.

As I relax, Carter wraps me in a blanket and carries me out of the room and into a room across the hall.

"Drink some water," he says, handing me a bottle.

"Even though I had plans to take you upstairs for the night, now I think I want to take you back to your place where we can be alone."

"Well, until Skye gets home," I say.

"Nope. We have the place to ourselves for the weekend. I gave Skye the keys to my place and full use of my butler. Right now, she is living it up," he says, chuckling.

"Why would you do that?" I ask, completely confused.

"You seem safe in your place, and it's comfortable for you. So, I would rather have you there than stress you out again, especially so soon. Skye was more than happy to spend the weekend at the penthouse. I scheduled a little mini spa day for her where they're coming in to give her a massage, a manicure and pedicure, and a facial. Trust me, she's having the time of her life, and I get you alone for the weekend in a space where I know you feel safe. That's a win-win in my book.

This man just gave up his penthouse apartment for the weekend to make sure that I was in a space where I felt comfortable.

He's making it hard to keep emotions out of our agreement.

Chapter 23

Carter

After we left the club and came back to her place, sex was more like it was the other night. It wasn't just fun at the club, but it was us connecting. I realized that I wanted more with her.

I want more than the contract, and I want to do things the right way. I want to show her I'm serious about all of this. Since I'm wide awake, I get up and make breakfast and get some thinking done.

By the time the food's ready, she's still asleep in bed. Making her a plate, I find a little tray in the cabinet and bring her breakfast to bed. After setting the tray on her nightstand, I gently sit on the bed and rub her arm to wake her up.

"Sweetheart, breakfast is here," I say.

Hearing my words, she rolls over onto her back and does that adorable little stretch she does in the morning that I love. Then she opens her eyes to look at me.

"Good morning," she smiles but then looks over at the tray of food.

"You made breakfast?" She sits up.

"Yep, I figure breakfast in bed will hopefully make up for the fact that I have to go out for a few hours today. We'll plan something to do when I get back. Okay?"

"It's fine. And thank you for breakfast," she says as she takes a bite of bacon. Then adds some salt to her eggs.

Grabbing my stuff, I take a quick shower and get dressed. I kiss her once more before heading out.

While I hate to leave her, I want to make sure I do things right before I move forward with her. I want her to know that I was listening when she talked and would always do what's best for her.

Making the drive across town, I follow my GPS to the address that I had Hunter find me. I'm certain I'm doing the right thing, but once I pull into her dad's driveway, nerves hit me.

Walking up, I knock on the door, and a woman about Gemma's age answers. She instantly hesitates when she sees me.

"You must be Summer. I'm Carter. Is your husband here?"

"Carter, as in the guy that Gemma has been spending time with?" she asks.

"Yes, that's me."

She doesn't move or say anything; she just stares me down with no emotion on her face.

"Stay here," she closes the door in my face.

I don't blame her. If the situation was reversed, I wouldn't want Gemma inviting some strange man into our place, either.

When I think about the fact that maybe someday we could have our place together, a huge smile covers my face. I've liked having her in bed with me every night, falling asleep beside her, and waking up to her. But we'll have to get out of that apartment sooner or later; it's too small.

Hopefully, we can find some place where she feels safe so that we can make it ours together. My mind starts racing with all these plans. I have to remind myself that I've got to slow down, and today is the first step.

When the door opens again, this time, Knox is standing on the other side.

"Is Gemma okay?" Are the first words out of his mouth.

"She's fine. I'm here to talk to you and possibly your wife, too." The look on his face goes from concerned to emotionless.

He's a powerful businessman like me, and he's learned to hide his emotions, which is what has made him so successful.

"Come on in," he opens the door and invites me into the formal living room right off the front door.

I take a seat in a chair, and he sits across from me on the couch with his wife pulled to his side.

"Gemma and I have talked, and I know how close she is with the two of you and how important you are in her life. So, when I started thinking about this, it only felt right to come and talk to you. I'd like to have your permission to officially date her. No contract, none of that. Just an actual relationship." I get the words out before I choke and suddenly feel like a teenage boy sitting there hoping I'm good enough to date my high school crush.

"Have you talked to her about this?" Knox asks.

"Not officially. We've gone out to dinner, but I haven't had this discussion with her."

"So, she may not even want this," Knox says.

"Knox!" Summer elbows him and gives him a glare.

"Sweetheart, she's my daughter. I'm always going to be protective," he retorts.

"And she's my best friend. She's talked to me about him more than she's talked to you. More than she'd ever be comfortable talking to you," Summer answers back. Then they lock eyes for a moment, having one of those silent conversations that only married couples can have.

"And what about the contract?" Summer asks.

Since they're friends, I figured she'd know and was probably one of the people that she talked to about the contract.

"We won't need it anymore. It's not like we've been following the rules of the contract, anyway. Her limits would still stand unless she wished to change them. I'd still always make sure that she's safe. But in order to get to know each other, we would date and spend time outside of Club Red."

Summer looks over at Knox, but he doesn't say anything.

"Listen, I'm sure I'm not who you wanted for your daughter. In the past, I've put up a lot of walls because I have been hurt a lot. Without even trying, your daughter has pushed past those walls and showed me that she doesn't care about my scars or the person I was in the past. All she cares about is who I am now. When she opened up and trusted me with things like her memory of the car accident the day her mother died and the nightmares and therapy she had had, I realized that we're not all that different. Her scars are on the inside; mine are on the outside. She's helping me heal in ways I never thought were possible. I like to think I'm helping her, too."

Again, neither of them says anything before Summer sighs.

"Knox, can I talk to you in the kitchen?" She stands and practically pulls him with her.

I don't know where the kitchen is in relation to this room, but I don't even hear mumblings or whispers. I know I did my best and hopefully pouring my heart out was enough to make them understand that I'm in this for the long haul. Maybe they'll be willing to give me their blessing because I know that would mean so much to Gemma.

After a few minutes, they come back and sit down in the same spots.

"As much as I hate to admit it, my daughter is an adult, and she can make her own decisions. I don't know you very well. I only know what I've heard about you and the little bit that you have shared with me. I never liked the idea of you and her together, especially with your history with the contracts. But if she opened up to you about that car accident, then I have to respect that you're someone she plans on keeping in her life," Knox says.

"She and I had been friends for a long time before she told me about what happened. Though she only did it because she had a nightmare one night when we were having a sleepover," Summer says.

"If you're willing to truly work at a relationship with her and you want more than just the contract, then based on how protective you have been with her during this whole Dustin situation, you have my approval for whatever it's worth," Knox says.

"Thank you, sir, and for the record, Dustin has taken a job on the other side of the country." I stare at him, trying to make my point.

Looking back at me, he says, "Mase?"

Since that's all he asked, I give a brief nod.

"What is Mase?" Summer asks.

"Nothing you need to worry about, sweetheart. Just know that Gemma is safe." Knox relaxes and kisses her temple.

"Now, with all this out of the way, I would like to have dinner with the two of you sometime in the near future. I would like to get to know you two as a couple. Talk to her to find out when she wants to do it." He stands and offers me his hand.

"Will do. And thank you," I say, shaking his hand.

He shows me out, and the entire drive back to Gemma's place, I have a huge smile on my face.

When I walk in, I find her dressed in jeans and a t-shirt with her hair tossed up in a messy bun on top of her head as she watches some reality show.

"Honey, I'm home," I joke.

Jumping up, she runs over, wrapping her arms around my neck. "I missed you."

I grip her ass, pull her up so she can wrap her legs around my waist as I move to the couch, and sit so she can straddle me.

"I wasn't gone all that long," I say, not able to take my hands off of her.

"I know, but I've gotten so used to you being here. When you leave, I don't know how I'm going to be able to stand it."

"Well, we'll just have to join a support group." I joke with her, and it feels good.

"So I had a very successful outing. I went and talked to your dad."

She freezes, looking at me. "About what?"

"About us. I wanted his blessing to take you out on a real date. It took some convincing, but he gave me his approval."

Her expression goes soft, and she melts against me.

"I can't believe you asked my dad."

"So now I'm going to ask you. Would you like to go on a date with me? A real, no contract involved date?" I ask.

"I guess that depends on what you have in mind?"

"Get dressed. Maybe something a bit dressy and shoes that are comfortable."

She hurries off and gets dressed. I keep her guessing the entire way until we pull into The Art Institute of Chicago.

She looks at me like I've lost my mind.

"Trust me. I have a plan."

We walk in with her hand in mine. Even though I've never been a big hand holder, I crave it with Gemma. As we enter I ask for a guy Gage told me to meet. We are greeted with friendliness and smiles.

Earlier, I had called and explained what I wanted. After giving them a substantial donation, they were more than happy to accommodate us.

"Mr. Morgan here tells us you love jewelry making. And you are a jeweler yourself?" The man says as we walk through the back hallways.

"Well, yes. I loved doing it with my mom. So when I went to college, I found a way to make a career out of it."

"Do something you love, and you will never work a day in your life. I love what I do here at the museum, so we are the lucky ones," he says.

Then he opens the door to one of the exhibits that have been blocked off for us.

"I think you will like this one the best. We should start over here with some of our Roman jewelry from the third century."

Her eyes go wide as she looks at me.

"I figure you can take some inspiration from some of the most famous pieces of jewelry history and make some of your own items."

She spends the next few hours engrossed in discussions with several of the staff who came to talk to her about different pieces and how they were crafted.

After spending time at the museum, we walked a few blocks to a chicken and donut shop she and Skye were talking about a few nights ago and had dinner.

When we got back to her place that night, she couldn't keep her hands off of me, and we barely make it to the bedroom. Picking her up, I place her naked body on the bed and climb over her. But she moves so fast, flipping me over on my back and climbing on top of me.

While I want to see where she is going with this, the moment she slides down my cock, I don't care. The slide at this angle feels incredible, but when her hands land on my chest, I react out of instinct and grip her wrists.

Our eyes lock, and she freezes her movements. I have to push away all old insecurities and know that I can trust her. Slowly, I let go of her wrists, move my hands to her hips and start moving her up and down on my cock.

When she gently explores my scars, if it wasn't that I can feel how wet and tight her pussy is, I wouldn't believe that she finds them in any way attractive.

But as she traces them, my brain only wants to focus on the pleasure of being inside of her, and my orgasm comes barreling at me hard. I stroke her clit because there is no way in hell I'm coming before she does. Thankfully, she doesn't make me wait.

As we lay in each other's arms trying to catch our breath, she snuggles up to me and places her head on my shoulder, still tracing the scars.

"Just in case I didn't make it clear tonight, I'm all in, Gemma. I want to toss the contract out the window. It's just you and me now."

"I want that too. But I'm scared."

"I know, but I'm not going anywhere."

Chapter 24
Gemma

So, after Carter kept me under a lock and key for a week, both Skye and Summer demanded a girl's night. I miss them both, so we agreed to meet at this Mexican restaurant that we've had many a girls' night dinner. They have delicious food and good margaritas.

The restaurant is a lively place filled with bright colors and the smell of Mexican dishes wafting through the air. There are twinkling lights hanging in the plants and festive decorations around the room. The corner booth we chose is big and comfortable, with enough room for all of us to settle in.

"Okay, Summer. First, how is married life?" Skye asks as we sip our first margaritas.

"It's still a little weird. I mean, I grew up in that house with sleepovers with Gemma. Yeah, and homework at the dining room table, staying up late and watching movies in the basement. Knox keeps asking me to decorate the house and put my touch on it. But I don't know. I feel like I should not touch anything," she says.

"Oh my God! Please decorate that house! Put color on the walls. Anything but white, for the love of God. Some throw pillows, maybe flowers would be nice. Even though I suggested it many times, it never happened because he is a man," I say.

Summer laughs, taking a sip of her margarita. "I know, I know. It's just weird to change everything so suddenly. But I'll work on it, I promise. Maybe you can come over one day, and we can kind of go over some ideas together. That house feels like it's your house and I'm just staying there. I don't want to touch anything that means something to you," Summer says.

It's obvious that she's reticent on the subject. The whole she's married to my dad thing is going to take some time to navigate.

"Leave my room alone, and if you find anything of my mom's, put it in my room and I will find a place for it. I know my dad has some of her stuff stashed in a closet somewhere. Even though we don't talk about it, I don't want to get rid of any of it either."

"I can work with that." She's smiles at me, and seems more relaxed now.

"Good, now Skye, what have you been up to?" I ask.

"Well, since we're heading into summer break, I figure I want to take it easy."

"What she means is spending more time at Club Red," I say.

We all burst into giggles.

"Yeah, I don't use my dad's allowance for the membership. It would be so much easier to just live off of what my dad gives me instead of working and going to school. So I figure I might as well make use of the membership because I doubt I'll be able to afford it once I graduate."

"Don't think like that! You're going to become some bad bitch girl boss and make tons and tons of money," Summer says.

"Cheers to that!" Skye shouts.

"Okay, Gemma, your turn. What's going on with Mr. Hunky Club Owner who decided you're the one girl to toss the contract away for?" Summer asks.

"Things have been going well. We've decided to take it slowly when we're at Club Red. Act as if nothing has changed. But outside of Club Red, everything's different. He is always texting and calling and taking me out on dates. Not just dinner, but actual dates where we can bond and do stuff together."

"So, it's the perfect relationship. You get your kinky needs met when you have your time at the club, and then you have a super-hot billionaire spoiling you the rest of the time," Skye says.

"Not to mention he's super protective and took care of the whole issue with Dustin," Summer adds.

"Yeah, he is pretty perfect," I say, smiling. "To be honest, taking this chance with him is terrifying. I'm more open with him than I have been with anyone before. It's one thing to open up about my past and what happened with my mom, but opening up about the stuff that we do at Club Red on top of it."

"It makes you more vulnerable," Summer says.

"Yeah, and that's terrifying," I agree.

"It's okay to be scared. It means you're pushing yourself out of your comfort zone. But don't make decisions based on that fear, and don't let the fear control you," Skye says, taking my hand.

Taking a deep breath, I nod. "You're right. I can't let fear control me. And honestly, Carter makes me feel safe and loved. I don't want to let that go."

"Then don't," Summer says. "You deserve to be happy, Gemma. You deserve to have someone who treats you right and makes you feel good."

I smile gratefully at my friends, feeling warmth spread through me. "Thank you, guys. I'm lucky to have you both."

"Alright, things have gotten way too serious here. This is supposed to be a fun girls' night out. No more depressing topics," Skye says refilling everybody's glass with the pitcher that they brought us. The smell of the lime in the margarita is so strong, I can almost taste it.

We spend the next two hours talking and eating, exchanging stories about our summer vacations. We laughed about the silly things we did as kids, the mischief Summer got into, and the tricks I played.

As the night goes on, the restaurant gets busier, and the music gets louder. Our laughter echoes through the walls as we indulge in more margaritas and chips and salsa. The atmosphere is electric, and I feel grateful for the happiness my friends bring into my life.

Then Summer's phone goes off and she pulls it from her purse.

"Oh, that's me. Knox and I are spending some time at Club Red tonight, so I've got to go. He's waiting for me outside." She winks, gives us a hug, and heads out.

After Summer leaves, Skye and I continue to chat and finish our drinks. It's been a while since we've had a girls' night out, and it feels good to catch up with her.

"Skye, don't look, but the blonde guy at the bar is checking you out," I say.

Smiling, she casually turns to get a good look at him. Then she does this flirting thing with her eyes, and before we know it, the guy is coming over.

"Would you like to dance?" He holds his hand out to Skye and she looks over at me.

I know she wants to know if it's all right if she leaves me by myself.

I shoo her off. "Go dance and have some fun."

The guy leads her out to the dance floor, where they dance for a few songs. She's constantly laughing and has a huge smile on her face.

I watch them dance for a while, feeling happy for Skye. It's clear that she's having a good time, and I'm glad that she's able to let loose and enjoy herself.

After a while, Skye comes back to the table to gather her things. "So, we're going to leave and do a little bar hopping. Are you okay to get home?"

"Yep, I'm calling a ride now. I plan on going home and having an early night because I work tomorrow."

Skye hugs me, and then she's off. I decide to wait on the sidewalk for my ride, that's still about fifteen minutes away. But no sooner do I step outside than a flash of lightning fills the air, followed by the crackling of thunder. Then it starts pouring down rain.

Rain is hammering down like bullets from a machine gun on the street, cars, and buildings. People are running for cover. Thunder crashes with the force of a hundred drums, and the sound leaves a lasting echo in the air. I can feel it in my chest and the ground beneath me. It's like a fist of fear that hits me.

Instantly, I flashback to that night of my mom's accident, and my heart races. Right now, I know there's no way I can get in the car with some stranger driving. Trying to take a few deep breaths, I go back into the lobby of the restaurant, sit down, and call Carter. Even though I know he said he had some work to catch up on; he's the first person I think of calling.

"Hey, sweetheart. How's your night? Are you having fun with your friends?" he asks.

"I was going home, and they've left. But it's thundering and lightning, and I can't get in the car with a stranger in the weather, and I don't know how I'm going to get home," I blurt it out so fast that I'm shocked he can understand me.

"I didn't even realize it was going to rain tonight. Stay where you are. I'm on my way, and I'll be there in about twenty minutes."

Just hearing his voice, I start to relax and calm down.

Then I get on my phone, cancel my ride, sit there, and wait. Twenty minutes come and go, and the rain starts pouring down harder. He's probably just going slowly in the rain. He will be here, I tell myself. Another thirty minutes go by with not a word, so I text him, and still nothing.

When another twenty minutes pass, and my phone rings, I jump, thinking it's him. Something held him up at the office, and he's calling to apologize and let me know he's on his way now.

Only it's Dad calling, and my stomach sinks.

Something is wrong. I know it before I even pick up the phone.

Chapter 25
Carter

Lately, some of these members have lost their minds. They think because they have money and throw money at us, we will turn the other cheek. We never have, and we especially can't now with this whole photo leak going on. Also, we're not telling them that because we don't need them to panic.

The latest one, I had to show him no mercy. He brought in a girl on her eighteenth birthday. Club Red is strictly twenty-one and over due to licensing. The worst part is the member knew it and brought her in with a fake ID.

Of all people to point this out was her mom, who was here at the time. Except the girl's mother was here cheating on her dad. The two of them had a huge blow-up scene. Thankfully, once they were removed, no one cared. Those members seemed to like drama.

Since Gemma is having a girls' night with her friends, I decided to do some security tests. So I'm sitting in the security office helping watch over things.

My gut is yelling at me. What for? I'm just not sure. Something isn't right, and I've been on high alert. Tonight I called a few extra security guys, offering to pay them double to work, and they agreed.

I'm not taking any chances. So, I decided to take a walk on the floor. Not wanting to sit behind a security camera all night; instead, I prefer to be on the floor, making my presence known.

As I enter the main room, the lights are low, but the energy is high. After scanning the room, I find Gage at the bar, so I go over to talk to him.

"Hey man, I haven't seen you in here in a while. Outside of meetings, of course."

We walk out of the main room and back toward the hallway leading toward the offices.

"Yeah, I was busy this year trying to prove myself with the new course I'm teaching, so I had many late nights. Plus, to be honest, this whole photo leak has me spooked. I haven't spent much time in the public areas," he says, looking around to make sure no one will overhear us.

"You and me both. All night we have been doing security drills, making sure there are no holes in the system to worry about," I tell him.

"Good. Oh, and I'm sorry. Missed the drama earlier. Jax told me about it. Seems like people got a good laugh from it."

"Yeah, because they don't know we are on high alert to prevent anything or anyone slipping through."

"That is why you are more stressed than normal. You need to get your girl in here for some relief."

"She's out with her friends tonight. Lots of catching up to do, apparently."

"So go be ready to spoil her when she is done."

The idea doesn't sound half bad. I hate the idea of not seeing her tonight.

"Hey, you two. Hiding out?" Sawyer says, walking up.

"Yeah, kind of," Gage says.

"Listen," I say. "I've been keeping my ear to the ground. What they've managed to dig up isn't enough to do anything to Club Red. Let's not give them a reason. We are on the radar of a few departments, and that is not where we want to be. So, no more slip-ups."

"Do you think someone would try to set us up?" I ask, and then tell him about the underage girl the member brought in tonight.

"No, they wouldn't go that far this soon. It would have the whole case thrown out. But I would put a halt on new members and guests if this continues. Though if they move forward on this, they will try to get someone in here," Sawyer says.

"Should we do that now?" I ask, starting to worry.

"As long as nothing else leaks and this is filed somewhere, no one is going to look at it again. That is until attention is brought to the club again," Sawyer says.

"No wonder those of us on the third floor have been using our private rooms," Gage says.

"You aren't wrong there," Sawyers says before leaving our group.

"Go have some fun. I'm going to get some work done," I say to Gage. Then head back to my office.

My office is one of the places in the building where I can have my cell phone. After checking it, I see nothing new.

Getting back to work, I go through my emails and wait for the report from the next security check we are doing. I lose myself in emails until my phone goes off. Seeing on the caller ID it's Gemma, I smile. I'm always happy to hear from her.

"Hey, sweetheart, how's your night? Are you having fun with your friends?" I ask while saving the email I was working on so I can give her my full attention.

"I was getting ready to leave, and they've left, and it's thundering and lightning, and I can't get in the car with a stranger in this weather, and I don't know how I'm going to get home."

She's speaking so fast, trying to get it all out. I can hear the panic in her voice. Already I'm standing and gathering my stuff.

"I didn't even realize it was going to rain tonight. Stay where you are. I'm on my way. I'll be there in about twenty minutes," I say as I'm walking out the door. I pass Gage on my out.

"Hey, what's wrong?" He asks, stopping in front of me.

"Gemma has this thing with rain, and she was out with friends. She just called me needing a ride home, but I can tell she's upset," I tell him.

He turns and starts walking with me.

"Remember to praise her that she called and did the right thing."

Gage has always been good about reminding not just me but the others too to praise when our subs do the right thing.

"I will. Just need to get to her first. Today when I checked, I didn't see any rain in the forecast. Since I know it's an issue for her, I've been watching out for it." Though I wonder if maybe I checked the wrong day.

"There wasn't any mention of rain. I watched the news getting ready this morning." He tells me like he knew what was going on in my head.

We stop when we reach the lobby.

"Thank you. Will you find Hunter and let him know what is going on and ask him to finish the last of the security drills tonight?" I ask, remembering I still had a few more to do.

"Yep, you got it. I saw him up in the third-floor lounge, so I'll head there now."

"Thank you." I go right to my car, get all my stuff in, making sure the front seat is ready for Gemma so she won't have to be standing in the rain waiting on me.

Then I plug in the address she gave me and double-check it with her tracker. They lined up, so I left.

The rain is coming down pretty hard for a storm that's come out of nowhere and no one knew it was going to rain. Turning onto the main road, I am sitting at the light, waiting for it to turn green when I pull up the voice control for my phone.

"Text Gemma," I tell it.

"What would you like to text Gemma?" it asks.

"I'm on my way, sweetheart. Just hang..."

A bright light fills my rearview mirror as the traffic light turns green. I don't even get my foot off the brake before the vehicle hits my car, and my world goes spinning.

Chapter 26

Gemma

"We shouldn't have gone out for a girls' night. I knew we shouldn't have." I say as I pace back and forth in the fluorescent-lit hospital waiting room.

The bright blue chairs line the walls in a neat row, and the smell of sanitizer, antiseptic, and bleach fills the air. The stark white walls contrast against the yellowing linoleum floor, and the fluorescent lights buzz incessantly above.

The room is sparsely filled with a few people here and there. Some are talking in hushed tones. Others are staring blankly into space. Now and then, a nurse or doctor will enter the room to call out a name or two, only to be met with silence.

Time stands still here, each minute feeling like an hour and every second stretching out endlessly before me. It's enough to give me a headache, not to mention keeping my mind spinning.

"None of us knew it was going to rain. If we did, we would have had a girls' night in and would have done it at our house, so you could have stayed the night in your room." Summer walks over, wrapping her arms around me.

As soon as my dad and Summer got to Club Red, they heard from Hunter about Carter's accident. Immediately my dad called me; they turned around to pick me up and take me to the hospital.

Ever since I got the phone call from my dad, I've been numb. I don't know how long I sat there waiting for them to pick me up or even which hospital we are at. It's a big blur and doesn't feel real.

"These are some of the best doctors in the area, and I'm sure they're checking him over for some minor issues. Though I doubt there was anything big, otherwise he would be in surgery," Dad says.

If I were thinking rationally, I might agree with him. But with every minute feeling like an hour, I don't think he's right. What I think is that Carter is on the verge of dying, and maybe he already has, and they don't know how to tell us.

I hate hospitals, and I avoid them at all costs. I'm trying to distract myself from the fact that I'm in a hospital that looks and smells an awful lot like the same one I was in the night that changed my life.

Finally, a nurse walks out, scanning the waiting room before she speaks.

"Gemma?" she asks.

"That's me," I say. I rush over to her faster than she expected because she takes a step back.

"Carter is fine. He's a little loopy right now due to some of the medication they gave him. But he's asking for you."

I should feel immediate relief that he's fine, but I don't. I'm still anxious, and my heart is racing.

"My dad and stepmom are coming with me," I say, not giving her any room to argue. In an instant, they are right at my side. There is no way I can do this without them.

We follow the nurse through several hallways, all with the same fluorescent lighting and the same smells as the waiting room. The only difference is the beeping that comes from each room as we pass.

She stops in front of a door, turning to look at us.

"Keep the lights dim. The bright lights hurt his eyes, and be careful of the wires. The doctor will come in a little bit to check on him and talk with you," she says, walking off.

Summer wraps her arm around my waist, giving me a side hug before I step hesitantly into the dark room. I'm unsure of what I'm going to see. When I get my first look at Carter, I stop in my tracks.

He's lying in the hospital bed with the hospital gown on and so many wires attached to him. He has an oxygen mask going over his face and an IV hooked up to his arm.

Several wires go under his gown, and he looks to be asleep. When I take a few hesitant steps toward the bed, my shoe squeaks on the wax floor. The sound causes him to open his eyes slowly.

"Gemma," Carter sighs my name and holds a hand up to me.

Taking a step forward, I hold on to his hand like it's a lifeline. He's got a bandage on the side of his face, visible bruising even in the dark light on his arm, and several small scratches.

I don't know what to say, so I just stand there and stare at him. Then suddenly, I'm the scared little girl in the back seat, watching the car flip over and over. Instead of my mom in the front seat, this time, it's Carter that gets taken away from me because I let him get too close. Because I cared about him too much. My body starts shaking, and I can't stop it.

"Hey, sit down here," Dad says, helping me sit in a chair by Carter's bedside.

My eyes stare at our joined hands before I look back up at Carter, and our eyes lock. Then something inside me snaps.

"No, I can't do this. It's just like mom. I just can't." I drop his hand, turn, and run out the door.

I don't even know if I'm going in the right direction. I pass room after room until I turn down a hallway and finally see an exit sign. Before I can go charging out, an arm wraps around my waist. I tense, ready to fight whomever it is.

"Gemma, calm down. It's just me," Summer says. Her voice is gentle and calm, making me relax slightly.

"Take a walk with me. I'm starving. I want to see what they have to eat in the cafeteria. The nurse says it's open, and they usually have some amazing chocolate cake."

Tired, all I can do is nod.

Summer wraps her arm through mine, holding on tight as if she's afraid I'm going to run. Honestly, I don't know if I will or not. Thankfully, she doesn't try to talk, and the silence mixed with the noise of our shoes squeaking on the floor as we walk somehow calms me.

Once we get down to the cafeteria, the main area is closed, but some shelves have the chocolate cake that we were told about. Summer buys us both a slice, and we sit at one of the empty tables.

"When Knox and I got together, I was terrified. He's older than me, and one of my biggest concerns was how much time we were going to get together," Summer says, taking a bite of the chocolate cake.

Even though I do the same, I can't taste the cake.

"It was a very hard conversation to sit down and have. I told Knox about how I was feeling because I wasn't sure I could put it into words. I love him more than anything in the world. Not being with him, whether it's him being out of town or something happening and taking him away from me for good, terrifies me." Then she sets her fork down and reaches across the table, taking my hand in hers.

"We have no idea how long we will be together. It could be four weeks, four months, or four years. If the universe aligns, we still have the chance of having forty years together. We just don't know, and to be scared that it could only be four weeks and miss out on forty years would be the stupidest thing I could ever do."

"Summer, your situation is entirely different, and you know it." I push my plate away from me, no longer hungry for even chocolate cake.

Nodding, she says, "Everyone's situation is different. No two are the same. But I want to ask you this question, and you can get mad at me all you want. But I think as your best friend, I've earned the right and especially now, seeing as I'm family."

I know instantly I'm not going to like what she has to say.

"I never got to meet your mom, but she sounds like an incredible woman from what I've gotten to know about her. You lost her at a young age, but would you have rather been too scared to enjoy that time and not had any time with her, or are you happy you got the few years that you did with her?"

"What kind of question is that? Of course, I'd rather have what time I had with her. Those memories are the most important thing in the world to me."

There are some days that I wonder if those memories are actual memories or just videos that my dad would play. Or things he would tell me about her. But the thought of not even having those is too much to bear.

"I knew that's exactly how you would feel. Now imagine meeting the love of your life and being too scared that something could happen to take him away. Would you be willing to give up that kind of love or be able to have someone love you like that because of fear? You and Carter could go on and be together another forty years. Just like Knox and I could.

"You're probably right. But tonight proved my greatest fear. As soon as I get close to someone, something happens, and they're going to be taken from me. This time, I got lucky. It's better for him that I walk away. Even though it'll hurt. But if I walk away, he can live a long and happy life. Knowing that will make it a little bit easier." Standing, I walk away, much more levelheaded than I was earlier.

"If that's true, how do you explain your dad, and how do you explain me?" Summer says behind me.

I don't answer her. I continue walking and find my way to the front of the hospital, where I'm easily able to get a taxi and go home. When I get home, Skye is waiting for me.

"Oh my gosh, I did not expect you home so soon. How is Carter? Is everything okay? Do you need to go right back to the hospital? I can help you pack a bag," she fires off a bunch of questions.

"He's fine. He's alive. I'm not going back; I'm going to bed," I say.

"Babe, you're going to have to give me more than that. What happened? Did he break up with you?" she asks.

"I don't want to talk about it. But if you must know, I'm sure Summer will be happy to tell you. She witnessed the whole thing and even tried to talk me down before I left. I don't want to be alone, so if you can be quiet and not ask a million questions, I'd love your company tonight."

"You got it. Get ready for bed, and I'll close up everything and be with you."

All through college, there were many times when I didn't want to be alone, mostly during thunderstorms. Skye or Summer would lay in bed with me, not talking. I liked that they didn't needlessly fill the silence and understood that having another person lying there next to me was enough to make me know I wasn't alone.

Tonight, that's all I need to know. That I'm not alone. My mind is constantly racing, and I don't think I have it in me to answer questions for anyone else when I can't even answer the questions I have for myself.

I've always had a set path in my life. For the first time, I feel like I'm completely adrift with no direction and have no idea where I want to go from here.

That alone is the scariest thing I can imagine.

Chapter 27
Carter

As I watch her walk out the door, my whole world goes dark. Her words bounced around in my head.

No, I can't do this.

I had finally decided that I'm all in, and she walks away, justifying why I kept my boundaries. Proving that all this time, the contract was the way to go.

No, I can't do this.

Gently, I reach up and touch the bandage on the side of my face.

No, I can't do this.

I guess the scars aren't bad when you don't have to look at them directly every day. But knowing that I'll have one on my face that everyone will be able to see is going to be too much for everyone.

Gemma can say the scars don't matter all she wants when they are on my back and hidden ninety percent of the time. But when it's in her face one hundred percent of the time, it's going to be a different story. No wonder she walked out.

No, I can't do this.

What's the point anymore?

"This isn't Gemma. The girl that walked out of here just now wasn't my daughter. She's in shock. Give her some time to come around and process it all." Knox says as Summer follows Gemma out the door.

No, I can't do this.

The words still echo in my head, and I'm not going to try to fool myself, thinking there's still any hope for us.

"I'm not stupid. She took one look at me and realized this time she'd have to look at my scars all the time. Let's call a spade a spade, shall we?"

"Carter, you didn't see her in that waiting room. There's no way she's walking away. Let Summer talk to her. I guarantee you she just needs to process what's going on."

"You can leave. Might as well start getting used to being alone," I tell Knox.

"I'm not leaving. The last thing you need is to be alone."

"Suit yourself. But I'm going back to sleep," I tell him, closing my eyes as he sits down in the chair next to my bed.

I tried to fight thinking about Gemma. I don't want to see her face or her smile. Eventually, I drift off to sleep. Nurses come in and check on me, but I'm barely conscious, and I wonder what type of sleeping medicine they gave me. By the time I'm fully awake, the sun is filtering in my room. Instead of Knox sitting in the chair, it's Hunter.

"Thought you were going to sleep the whole day away, Sleeping Beauty." He says when he notices that I'm awake.

"Might as well. It's not like there's anything left to do," I grunt. Then I slowly move the bed to a sitting-up position to check out the breakfast that's on the table next to me.

"Knox filled me in on what happened last night, and I tend to agree with him. You have got to let her process everything. There's a lot she needs to think about."

"If that's what you think, so be it," I say, not believing him.

All night I heard those words. In my dream, it was like I was chasing them down through a dark room, trying to find her on the other end, and she kept getting further and further away.

No, I can't do this.

I think those words will haunt me for the rest of my life. Right now, I don't know how I'm going to escape them. Maybe in time I'll forget them, but right now, it's just too much.

As I eat the cold pancakes, slightly runny scrambled eggs, over-cooked toast, and undercooked bacon, Hunter goes on and on about stuff going on with Club Red. I'm sure his intention is to take my mind off of things.

Only I don't hear a word he says. To be honest, I couldn't care less. As I'm finishing eating, a doctor in a white lab coat steps in followed by what I assume is a nurse behind him.

"Hello, Mr. Morgan, I'm Doctor Alvarez. I'm here to take a look and see what I can do to minimize that scar on your face." The doctor walks over to me with a warm smile lighting up his face.

Why wouldn't he be smiling? He doesn't have a blemish on his skin. He's still young enough to get any girl that he wants and add that doctor label, and families love him.

"What's one more scar?" I push the rolling table with a plate of food to the side.

"Come on; it's not going to be that bad. Let me take a look. From the notes left last night from the doctor, I'm pretty sure they'll be next to no scarring." He moves closer to me to examine the wound.

"Carter let him take a look," Hunter says in his no-nonsense tone.

I'm not used to being told what to do. I'm the one that gives the orders, I'm the one in charge, and I don't like this dynamic shift one bit.

I cross my arms over my chest and look over at the doctor, who hesitantly reaches up and pulls the bandage off my face.

"Oh yes, they put on some liquid glue. But I can use some superfine sutures and stitch this up to the point that you'll be able to see very little of this scar outside the hairline. I can go ahead and get this done today," the doctor says.

Opening my mouth to say no, Hunter beats me to it.

"That sounds great. Go ahead," Hunter says. Then he glares at me, daring me to disagree with him.

It doesn't matter anymore to me. But it seems to matter to him, so I nod my head to let the doctor do his thing. Hunter doesn't leave my side, and every time the doctor asks me a question, my response is the same. Do whatever you want.

So, Hunter pretty much takes over. After the doctor leaves and I have a fresh bandage on my numb face, Hunter finally unleashes on me.

"I get it that you have given up, but you need to get it the fuck together. You don't believe anyone when we tell you that Gemma just needs time. Do you ever think maybe she feels guilty about all this? That maybe this is her fault because she called you? And really, what does it say for the two of you if you're going to let her walk out that door so fucking easily? If she isn't for you, maybe this is a sign that there is someone out there, and you're going to fuck it all up with this thinking. Why? I don't care. If I have to drag you back into the land of the living, kicking and fucking screaming, I will. I'm going to be a thorn in your side until you get your shit together," he says. With that, he stands and walks out the door.

He's probably heading out to find food, and I don't doubt that he will be back. Even though I might be ready to give up, I know Hunter won't.

But Hunter was right about one thing, he is going to have to drag me kicking and screaming.

Chapter 28

Gemma

After one night in my bed, I couldn't stand to be there anymore. So, I came home. For the first time since Dad and Summer got together, I spent the night in my childhood room.

They've left it just the way I had it. Walking in here feels like stepping into a huge hug. I still didn't sleep great, but I was at least at peace being here.

I have no idea what time it is because I left my phone downstairs after a long conversation with Pink. I wanted to know how to end adynamic and the best way to go about it, especially when a contract is in place.

So after a long-wrenching phone call, I left my phone plugged in on the kitchen counter, not wanting to deal with anyone who was calling. If someone needed me, they could call my dad. But judging by the bright morning light coming through my window and the smell of coffee and bacon drifting upstairs, I guess that I should get up.

Using the attached bathroom, I wash my face, pull my hair back into a messy bun, and slip on some sweatpants instead of the shorts that I slept in. Then I go downstairs.

Hesitantly, I walk into the kitchen, not sure what I'm going to find. But the sight brings tears to my eyes because it's something I have imagined for so many years. Summer is at the stove cooking breakfast, and Dad is sitting at the kitchen island with a cup of coffee in front of him, reading the newspaper.

I'd always hoped he'd find a woman that would take care of him. But more than that, I wanted a typical family. While it may be unconventional since Summer is my age and my best friend and now my stepmom, I think that I got my dream in a very untypical way.

"Hey, sweet pea, how did you sleep?" Dad asks once he notices I'm standing in the kitchen.

"Not great. But better than at my place." I walk over and pour myself a cup of much-needed coffee. When I turn towards the refrigerator, Summer has already grabbed my favorite coffee creamer and is handing it to me.

"So, I made that blueberry French toast casserole that you like. It's almost done, and so is the bacon." She pulls the last of the bacon off the skillet and places it on the dish with the paper towel. "You go sit down. I'll bring this stuff over."

I follow my dad to the table. He took his seat at the head of the table, and I took mine to his right but then hesitated.

"That's your seat. Summer sits on this side. Nothing's changed." My dad says with a smile as we sit down.

"In all fairness, things have changed. She finally put your damn golf clubs away and decorated the entranceway and added some damn color to the living room, like I have been begging you to for years." I joke with him like I normally would, and that causes him to laugh.

"Wait until you see what she's done with the basement," he says.

"Well, we had both been hounding you for years to put some color in the place. Now I have an excuse to do it. Gemma and I had an entire plan for what we would do to this house if we could. I just get to be the one to execute it." Summer kisses the top of my dad's head before getting the casserole out of the oven.

It's easy to see how truly happy they are. It's in everything that they do. Summer might have cooked breakfast and set it on the table, but my dad fills her plate first before allowing me to get my food and then taking his last.

They keep the topics at breakfast light. But I watch how he's so attentive over her, filling up her water before it's empty and adding more bacon to her plate when she eats the last of it. Then serving her a second helping of French toast.

I'm so happy for both of them, and the fact that I get to have them in my life means the world to me. Maybe someday I can find the same, but I don't know if it's in the cards for me.

"How did you get over Mom?" I ask when there's silence between conversations. At some point, he had to have gotten over her. Otherwise, he couldn't be this happy with Summer. I don't think I thought about what I just asked.

But I notice the look that he and Summer are sharing as he tries to answer the question.

"I think we should talk. Why don't we go to the basement?" he asks.

"I've got the dishes, and then I think I'm going to go hang out by the pool. That's where I'll be if you guys want to join me when you're done," Summer says.

Not sure what to make of it all, I follow my dad to the basement.

There's a large, oversized couch in front of the TV down there. It's decorated in lots of colors, but I don't see them. All I can think about is what's so important that has to be said down here.

Once we get seated, I wait for my dad to speak. But he looks extremely uncomfortable.

"For the record, what I'm about to tell you, Summer and I already had this talk before we got married. But I had asked her not to tell you since I had made your mom a promise. So don't be mad at her.

She's toeing a tough line between being your best friend and being my wife."

"I promise I won't be mad at her. I know your relationship has changed, and she's holding secrets from you about me as well."

My dad glances at me before looking down at his hands again.

"Your mom and I were high school sweethearts. You know that. I had made your mom a promise. She wanted you to have a normal fairy tale childhood. One that she didn't get. So even after she died, I kept the promise, and I thought nothing of it until now. I pray that she'll forgive me for shattering the illusion."

"What are you talking about?" My mind is racing. What illusion is he worried about shattering?

"The part about your mom and I being high school sweethearts is true. When she ended up pregnant, we got married because that was the right thing to do at the time. Unfortunately, by the time you were born, we realized we were more friends who had a child together than anything else. In the hospital room, while I was holding you for the first time, she made me promise I would never tell you that we were anything less than soul mates. We made it work for you. I took care of both of you, and if your mother were alive, I'd be taking care of her still."

Sitting there, I let what he says settle in and something in the back of my head clicks.

"But you wouldn't be happy."

He looks at me again; gives me a tense smile before looking away. Though he never answers me.

"You were six when your mom was killed in that car accident. The fact that I couldn't grieve for her like she deserved weighed on me for many years. I was more thankful that you survived than I was upset at losing her. But I made a vow at her funeral that I would not remarry until you were at least eighteen. I would not let you see me date or see anything that would tarnish her memory until you could understand. So, then I found Club Red. It was enough for me. I didn't feel the need to date or have anyone serious. Instead, I was focused on raising you. Don't forget you were a bit of a wild child and a handful."

He's not lying. I was a risk-taker in school and liked pushing my boundaries. But it was only because I felt safe with him.

"So, to answer your question, there was nothing really to get over other than the grief that I wasn't able to mourn her the way she deserved. That lessened with time and a little therapy."

"I never knew you went to therapy, Dad."

"Really? I thought you had figured it out. If you had ever asked, I would have said it was to help with grieving your mom, which wasn't a lie. It just wasn't the way that you would have thought."

Getting up, I go over and hug him.

"Growing up after Mom died, I had dreams of a normal family. Things that I saw other people in school doing that I wouldn't be able to do. More than anything, from the time I was in middle school on up, I was hoping you'd remarry. I wanted you to be happy. But I also thought that then I'd at least have a mother figure. Someone who could bake cookies to put in my lunch box with cute little notes, chaperone field trips, and have the awkward talks with me so you wouldn't have to. But another part of me was always glad to have you to myself, and I enjoyed every minute of it. Now I see how happy you and Summer are, and I'm glad you found each other, even if it's a little awkward at times."

He pulls me in for another hug and I think he's relieved not to have this secret between us. Since I've become an adult, we are more like friends, and I hate that he felt like he had to hide this for so long.

"Now, as your father, I'm going to put my two cents in on this subject, and then I'm going to drop it. While you're here, I promise I will not bring it up again."

Immediately tensing, I scoot further from him because I know where this is going.

"If Summer hadn't shown up at Club Red, I never would have made a move or thought we could be anything more than friends," he says.

I pause because this is so not where I thought the conversation was going.

"But you told me that you loved her long before that."

"I did. But she was your best friend and way too young for me, and I never would have crossed that line. Even once we did get together, the fact that she was so much younger than me terrified me. I was worried that I was a passing amusement or that maybe I was just the creepy dad of her best friend, and she couldn't tell me no. I was worried she'd get bored with me and want a man her age. But most of all, I'm terrified of leaving her alone in this world."

I can hear the emotion in his voice, and it brings tears to my eyes. My dad's never been one to share his fears with me. He has always shouldered them himself to make my life easier.

"While I know we have many things ahead of us, this age gap will always make it more difficult. But I'll gladly face them with her at my side."

Then it clicks what he's trying to say. He's trying to talk about me and Carter.

"But I thought you'd be happy about this. You're pretty vocal that you didn't want us together."

My dad looks at me this time, and there's some guilt on his face.

"That's before I realized you loved him and that he loved you."

The words hit me like a sucker punch to the gut. It hurts so much I have to wrap my hands around my stomach and try to catch my breath.

Love? No. Lust? Definitely. But not love.

Dad moves to my side and pulls me in for another hug while I'm still trying to catch my breath.

"Life is about risks, and I thought you realized that because you were a risk taker. It scared the shit out of me sometimes, but you were living life, and that's all I wanted for you. Somewhere along the way, you stopped, and it's like you crawled into the shell that you haven't been able to find your way out of. You have taken no risks, and I can tell you right now, this is not what your mom would have wanted."

I tried to pull away, but he hugged me a bit harder. After a moment, I wrapped my arms around him too.

"You have to live. Living means that sometimes there's pain. Loving means that sometimes you open yourself up to heartbreak and trust that the person won't break your heart. Many nights, your mom and I were up at three in the morning while you were wide awake, and we would sit there and talk about our hopes and dreams for you. By that point, we were still trying to figure out how our dynamic would work. We were young and just out of high school. Her biggest wish for you was that you would find true love and someone that would love you with their whole heart and that you wouldn't be scared of it. She wanted what we knew we wouldn't have. We wanted to give you the life you deserved. Right now, I can tell you I want you to have what Summer and I have. And I don't want you to wait years, or decades before you have it."

For a moment longer, we hugged, and then he finally let go of me. My dad has given me a lot of advice over the years, and most of it is spot on.

Maybe I'll go talk to Carter, but I can't do it right now because I have no idea what the hell I'd say to him.

Chapter 29
Carter

I'm back at Club Red, sitting in my office, trying to get work done. Several people have popped their heads in to tell me that they were glad I'm back and ask how I'm doing. I know they care, and I appreciate it, but a big part of me wants to forget this ever happened.

After answering some emails, I look up to find Hunter and Gage standing there. They both take a seat in the chairs across from my desk.

I guess that Hunter told Gage what was going on at least in part. Normally, us founding members are close and tight-knit. We know what's going on in each other's lives. We're like our own little support system, but it's also important for the sake of Club Red.

"Alright, I told Gage about this bullshit of you letting Gemma go. He agrees with me that you're a fucking moron," Hunter says.

"Christ. Tell me how you feel." Then, saving my email, I give them my full attention.

"I have. You just don't listen. We could all see how much you two liked each other and how good you two were with each other. You can deny it all you want. She was more than just a contract, and what you had was more than just a dom and sub relationship. You got the real thing, and you're letting her go. Why?" Hunter asks.

Well, I could always count on him not to spare my feelings on anything.

"I'm not letting her go. She up and left. Said she couldn't handle it. It's one thing to have scars that she doesn't have to look at because I can cover them with clothes, but it's completely another thing to see a scar every time she looks me in the eye. I guess that was just too much for her. Not that I can blame her. It's too much for me to look myself in the eye."

"Carter, that is such bullshit. It is too much for some people, absolutely, but we all know Gemma is not like that. There's something else there and I'm guessing as her dom, you know what that is. Even if you don't realize it. And if you don't, you should be forcing her to talk about it because it's big enough to scare her this much. Stop the damn pity party and man the fuck up," Gage says.

Sitting there, I stare at him because this man so rarely cusses that I can't remember the last time that he did.

When I asked him about it once, he said that it's easier to be in the habit of not cussing instead of having to censor himself when he's in front of his classes, which makes sense.

So, the fact that not only did he cuss, but he said fuck caught my attention.

"This isn't the Carter I know. Even when you were injured, you didn't give up like this. You fought, and you fought hard because you had something to live for. Even before Gemma, you had something to live for. One girl doesn't wipe that all that way, regardless of what happened. So, I agree with Gage's sentiments. Go home and don't come back until you man the fuck up. Because you're not any use here otherwise," Hunter says, completely serious.

With that, they both stand and walk out of the room. I'm left there slack-jawed, staring after them, wondering what universe I've been transported to. Then one of the security guys steps in.

"Hunter gave orders that I am to escort you off the property," he says.

The poor guy looks uncomfortable, not that I can blame him.

This isn't his fault, and I'm not getting him in trouble.

"Hunter knows me all too well. While he knows I won't listen to him, he knows I won't put you in the middle, either. He's a fucking evil genius bastard." I say partly under my breath. But it earns me a chuckle from the security guy whose name I'm not quite sure of.

So, gathering my things, I let the guy walk me to the front door. He stands there and watches me get in my car and leave the parking lot. There's still plenty of work I can do from my office at home. Mostly getting on top of all my damn emails so that I can be productive the next time I'm allowed back at the club.

Gemma wasn't here much, but I can still see her in every space. I gave her that stupid tour, so she got to see every room. There's no place that I can hide in my own house.

After pouring myself a glass of whiskey, I sit on the balcony and watch the city move on without me. I spend so much energy trying not to think about Gemma that about the time I finish my glass, I'm exhausted. Then I get ready for bed, hoping that sleep will be a sweet escape from all this.

As I lie in bed with my eyes closed, no matter how hard I try, all I see is Gemma. I run over what I could have done differently. Why did she leave? We barely talked at the hospital.

Maybe when I talked to her on the phone, I could have said something different. Or maybe my plan should have always been to pick her up from girls' night. Then something in my brain clicks, and I sit up straight in my bed in the middle of the dark room.

After the car accident, she was with her mom, and it was raining. She called me that night because it started raining. Because she couldn't stand the rain and she didn't trust some stranger to drive her home. So, she called me because she trusted me.

What I saw on her face that night wasn't disgust for my scar. It was fear. Pure fear. Then in my mind, I hear those words yet again. But this time, I hear the ones that came after them too.

No, I can't do this. It's just like Mom. I just can't.

Our conversation over what happened with her mom comes flooding back to me. What courage it must have taken my girl to walk through the doors of that ER. To wait in that waiting room and then walk into that room where I was in that bed.

The similarities of the accidents hit her hard. She couldn't handle it, but it had nothing to do with my scar. I don't know how I could ever think that, anyway. Because ever since she's been able to see and touch my scars, they've done nothing but turn her on.

What a fucking idiot I am. How the hell did I block that out? When I check the time, it's just after nine p.m., so I throw on my clothes and grab my keys.

Driving on autopilot, I arrive at her father's house. I walk up and knock on the door. It takes a minute, but her dad answers.

"She's not here. Summer and Skye are at her apartment," he says flatly.

"Good. Because I didn't come here to talk to her, I came here to talk to you."

He continues to stare at me, and I hope he understands my meaning.

"Then I guess you should come on in," he steps aside and then closes the door behind me.

Chapter 30
Gemma

It was nice to get together with Summer and Skye at the apartment and just be. They didn't ask questions or try to talk about Carter. Instead, we talked about work and watched some movies. Then caught up on social media, binged on junk food, and then, like little kids, we made a pillow fort in the living room. Finally, we fell asleep.

That's why it takes me a few minutes to orient myself when I wake up to someone banging on the door.

"Is it the cops? Should we try to contact a hitman?" Skye mumbles without even opening her eyes.

"If it was the cops, they'd be yelling *police*," I grumble. Then I get up as Summer hasn't even budged from the noise. I'm feeling a little upset that I'm the one having to get up, so I give her a solid nudge with my foot before walking to the front door.

Whoever is on the other side starts pounding again. Being that I haven't even had coffee, and it's barely daylight out, I'm starting to get pissed.

"We're not fucking emergency services. Call 911. What are you doing up so fucking early?" I yell. When I open the door, I'm shocked to find Carter on the other side.

Even though he doesn't look like he's slept much, he's in his classic everyday suit and up and walking. Not in the hospital bed anymore. My eyes go to where the bandage was on his face, and there's a small scar there. Honestly, it looks sexy as hell. My body doesn't realize we're supposed to be mad at him for waking us up so early because everything in me is attracted to him right now.

"Carter, what the hell?" I ask. Leaving the door open, I turn and go right into the kitchen for coffee. If I'm going to have it out with him, I need to be firing on all cylinders.

He steps in and closes the door behind him, and then looks around the room but doesn't say anything.

"Seriously, Carter, what the fuck?" Skye whines and pulls a pillow over her face.

"Carter's here?" Summer asks, still clearly confused.

"Just go back to sleep," Skye tells her.

This earns a chuckle from Carter before he turns back to look at me. I press the start button on the coffee machine that I had been preparing during their little back and forth.

"You look like you're doing well. How are you?" I ask, trying to make small talk.

"Good. A little sore still. I have a few bruises which are healing." He never takes his eyes off of me.

"We're going to go hang out in my room," Skye says. Then she and Summer pull blankets over them like sweaters and go down the hallway.

They make a good show closing the bedroom door, but they're probably listening in the hallway just in case I need them. What kind of friends would they be if they abandoned me at a time like this?

"I'm sorry it took me this long to come after you. I wish I had a better excuse other than I had a few things I had to work through myself," he whispers.

Though I want nothing more than to rush into his arms, I'm not quite sure what he wants yet.

"I'm the one who should be sorry. When you needed me the most, I abandoned you. I haven't checked up on you. Instead, I just completely dropped off the face of the earth. While I know you have no reason to believe me, I was going to give you a call today to see if you wanted to have lunch when you were feeling better," I say.

I haven't even told Summer or Skye yet, but I decided at some point last night before we all fell asleep. Part of me just needed to make sure that he was all right and that the last memory I had of him wasn't him in a hospital bed.

"Of course, I believe you. I would have said yes to lunch and insisted it be today so I could see you." He steps around the kitchen island and stands in front of me, too far away to reach.

"I freaked out and thought it would be easier and better to walk away. But it's not, and I don't want to walk away. I want whatever time we have together. However much longer you want to do the contract, that's what I want."

I hope against hope he still wants to spend time with me. Even if that time has an end date. After the way I acted, I don't dare hope that we can spend time outside of that contract.

"Oh, this contract?" he says, reaching into his inside jacket pocket and pulling out the folded-up paper and setting it on the counter.

I recognize the front page of the contract that we signed that night over dinner. Holding my breath, I wait to see what he says.

He looks over at it and then picks it up. "I don't want this contract anymore."

My heart sinks as I stand there and watch him rip the contract to shreds and set it back on the counter.

"I want something new." He looks up at me with a completely genuine smile on his face, one that I can see even in his eyes.

Then, reaching into his pants pocket, he pulls out a little velvet box and drops down to one knee. My mind doesn't register what's happening because, for some reason, I think he's leaning down to tie his shoe at a most awkward time.

"I want a lifetime contract with you. I want every morning and every night. I want to sleep with you in my arms, wake up, make you breakfast, and spend evenings cuddling on the couch. I want to enjoy Club Red with you and want to go buy a house and build a home together. Maybe someday start a family together. I want to be at your side and be the one helping you make all your dreams come true. I love you, Gemma. Will you marry me?"

That's when I finally look at the ring and realize instantly it is my mom's ring. I have faint memories of sitting on her lap and playing with it. One time she even let me put it in my hand, and I could imagine what it would be like to wear it when I was married. I hadn't even realized my dad had saved it.

"That was my mom's ring," I say, shocked.

"I went and talked to your dad last night. Until well after midnight we talked and he wasn't easy on, me making sure that I would be able to take care of you. That I wanted to marry you for the right reasons. In the end, he gave his blessing and gave me this ring to propose to you."

He talked to my dad. I mean, he talked to my dad for hours. That was something that didn't sit right with me with Dustin. My dad had no idea that Dustin had any intention of proposing because he never talked to my dad before or after.

"Hey baby girl, I asked you a question," Carter says, pulling my attention back to him. This time instead of a smile on his face, he looks nervous.

I wish I could drag it out and enjoy his nervousness for a bit longer, but as soon as it all clicks what's going on, full-on excitement hits me.

"Yes, of course, and I love you too!" I say. Then throw myself at him before he even gets a chance to put the ring on my finger.

He wraps me in his arms as he stands up and holds me tight before pulling back just enough to kiss me.

When his lips meet mine, I moan because it's been too long. To be honest, I didn't think I'd feel his kiss again, especially as I watched him rip up that contract.

His kiss is passionate and full of emotion. I can feel all the love he has for me in that one single kiss. His lips are soft and gentle as they move with mine. The heat of his mouth ignites a fire within me I hadn't felt before. His hands slide up my back and into my hair as we deepen the kiss. His tongue explores every inch of my mouth.

The kiss is over way too soon. He pulls back and slides the ring onto my finger. I look down at it and can't help but smile. It's a beautiful diamond-encrusted engagement ring with sapphires on either side. The diamonds sparkle in the light, and I can feel the warmth of the ring radiating from my finger.

I'm about to say something when I hear a gasp behind me and turn around to see Summer and Skye standing in the doorway, their jaws on the floor.

"You two were eavesdropping?" Carter asks with a smirk before turning back to me and leaning down for one more kiss.

We spend a few more minutes staring into each other's eyes before we finally break apart. Both of us smiling from ear to ear.

Summer and Skye come over, both of them talking at once as they give us hugs and congratulate us. We all stand there for what feels like hours, talking about our plans for the future.

I don't think I could have picked a more perfect day or moment if I tried.

Epilogue

Gemma

A few months later

My whole life, I've dreaded wedding dress shopping because that's something that your mom is supposed to do with you. Carter knows this, and he's gone above and beyond to make sure that this experience is something I will never forget and a very positive one.

My dad seems to understand too. He stepped into the role my mom would have taken during wedding planning. He's done it so seamlessly. The best part is he seems to truly enjoy it, and he's been having as much fun as Summer, Skye, and I have.

So, I have the three of them with me today, but I also have Carter's mom. We've gotten to know each other since the engagement. This is the first wedding event she's been to, and she's slowly opening up to me. I'm the first girl Carter has brought home since his ex dumped him when he was in the military.

Even though he's taking care of her, I'm learning that Carter's kept his mom at a distance because of Club Red. But we'll spend big holidays with her. Though he didn't see her every week, that's starting to change since our engagement. It's just a slow going process.

The girl who's helping me get dressed zips me into the last part of this dress. Then I step out into the viewing area where everyone waits. There are more mirrors than should be allowed in one place, and I can see myself from angles that should be illegal.

No one reacts because I've learned that they wait to see what I say first. I look at myself, but I also look at them in the mirror, and I can tell this is not the dress. Turning around to look at them, I shake my head.

"I liked the first dress on you better, Sweet Pea." My dad says, and both Summer and Skye agree with him.

"She looks beautiful in that dress, but I think the second dress you looked better. Didn't you?" Carter's mom adds.

"Yeah, but it still wasn't the one." Going back into the dressing room, I take this dress off and put on the next one.

Everyone's drinking champagne, and the conversation is flowing with everyone talking and enjoying themselves. I love that atmosphere here.

As I step out of the dressing room in the next dress, I don't even have to get into the mirrors. Everyone's opinion is all over their face. This is the dress. And when I step in front of the mirrors, my eyes water.

"Wow, I'm going to be a bride," I say as it finally sinks in.

"This is the dress." Summer says, and they all agree.

"This is the dress," I say.

My dad jumps up and hugs me.

"What does she need to go with the dress? Does she need a veil? Choose a corset? I don't know, but get her whatever she needs to go with it." My dad tells the girl who is helping me get dressed, and she scampers off.

After we're done fully accessorizing, I'm going back to put on my clothes when Skye drops a bomb.

"I slept with my professor at Club Red," she says, covering her face.

We are all silent.

"Let me get out of this dress, and then we'll talk," I tell her. I don't think I have ever gotten dressed so fast in my life.

"Okay, I'm starving. Let's grab food, but I'm going to have questions," I say. Then I text Carter, who said he was working in the area and would grab lunch with us.

He texts me back, telling me about a place a few blocks away. By the time we arrive, he's already there with a table for us.

"Hello, my love. Did you find your dress?" He greets me before talking to anyone else.

"I did. But my dress is not the topic of this conversation. Skye dropped a bomb on us."

We all sit down, and I look over at Skye, who's sitting next to me. Carter, who's sitting on the other side of me, wraps his arm around my waist as I take her hand in mine. Then, I ask her, "What happened?"

"I met this great guy at Club Red, and we had a few scenes together, and things were going great. Then school started, and this past Tuesday morning I'm in my class, and in he walks, my professor."

"Oh shit," Carter says beside me. "It's Gage, isn't it?"

"How do you know that?" Her eyes snap to Carter.

"He's a good friend of mine. A great guy. And he just had a meltdown today because he found out that he had slept with one of his students."

"Great. I finally met a good guy, and of course, the universe would throw me the curveball of a lifetime. He wouldn't dare risk his career to date a student. He's friends with my best friend's soon-to-be husband, who owns the club, and I'm the only person whose reputation stands to be ruined if this gets out. Plus, I'm losing my roommate, and I'm no longer looking forward to living alone. Not super important, but still sucks and worth throwing in there."

"I don't know what happened. But he says you ran out of that classroom so fast when class ended he hasn't gotten a chance to talk to you yet. Don't kill the messenger, but I think you should talk to him. At the very least, I think he might put your mind at ease. As far as living alone, our new house has a guesthouse, and you're welcome to it. That way, you're in your own space, and we're in our own space, but you're not alone," Carter says.

We had talked about letting Skye stay in the guesthouse because, as much as she was putting on a brave face, I knew she was not looking forward to being left on her own. Plus, if she's on the property, we can still make sure that she's safe. Carter didn't even hesitate when I brought it up. He just made it happen.

The guesthouse needed a bit of work. In two weeks, it was ready and surprisingly decorated to the Skye's taste.

When I look at my dad across the table, whatever he's thinking, his face doesn't give it away. I need to remember to ask his opinion on all this later. I know that he knows Gage too. Even though I haven't met him yet, I'm interested in my dad's opinion of the guy.

"You don't have to twist my arm about the guesthouse. But that doesn't fix everything. I've screwed up this time."

Want more Carter and Summer? Get a **bonus epilogue here!**

Ready for Skye's story? Grab it in **Forbbiden Dom!**

Other Books by Kaci Rose

See all of Kaci Rose's Books

Oakside Military Heroes Series

Saving Noah – Lexi and Noah

Saving Easton – Easton and Paisley

Saving Teddy – Teddy and Mia

Saving Levi – Levi and Mandy

Saving Gavin – Gavin and Lauren

Saving Logan – Logan and Faith

Saving Zane

Oakside Shorts

Saving Mason - Mason and Paige

Saving Ethan – Bri and Ethan

Mountain Men of Whiskey River

Take Me To The River – Axel and Emelie

Take Me To The Cabin – Pheonix and Jenna

Take Me To The Lake – Cash and Hope

Taken by The Mountain Man - Cole and Jana

Take Me To The Mountain – Bennett and Willow

Take Me To The Cliff – Jack

Take Me To The Edge – Storm

Mountain Men of Mustang Mountain

(Series Written with Dylann Crush and Eve London)

February is for Ford – Ford and Luna

April is For Asher – Asher and Jenna

June is for Jensen – Jensen and Courtney

August is for Ace – Ace and Everly

Club Red – Short Stories

Daddy's Dare – Knox and Summer

Sold to my Ex's Dad - Evan and Jana

Jingling His Bells – Zion and Emma

Club Red: Chicago

Elusive Dom - Carter and Gemma

Forbidden Dom – Gage and Sky

Chasing the Sun Duet

Sunrise – Kade and Lin

Sunset – Jasper and Brynn

Rock Stars of Nashville

She's Still The One – Dallas and Austin

Accidental Series

Accidental Sugar Daddy – Owen and Ellie

The Billionaire's Accidental Nanny - Mari and Dalton

The Italian Mafia Princesses

Midnight Rose - Ruby and Orlando

Standalone Books

Texting Titan - Denver and Avery

Stay With Me Now – David and Ivy

Committed Cowboy – Whiskey Run Cowboys

Stalking His Obsession - Dakota and Grant

Falling in Love on Route 66 - Weston and Rory

Connect with Kaci Rose

Website

Kaci Rose's Book Shop

Facebook

Kaci Rose Reader's Facebook Group

TikTok

Instagram

Twitter

Goodreads

Book Bub

Join Kaci Rose's VIP List (Newsletter)

About Kaci Rose

Kaci Rose writes steamy contemporary romances mostly set in small towns. She grew up in Florida but now lives in a cabin in the mountains of East Tennessee.

She is a mom to 5 kids, a rescue dog who is scared of his own shadow, an energetic young German Shepard who is still in training, a reluctant indoor cat, and 2 barn cats who she has to stop her kids from trying to pet constantly.

She also writes steamy cowboy romances as Kaci M. Rose.

Please Leave a Review!

I love to hear from my readers! Please **head over to your favorite store and leave a review** of what you thought of this book!

Made in USA - Kendallville, IN
19784_9781954409538
05.01.2024 1618